I0628994

Church Girls Just Want to Have Fun

A Christian Fiction Novel

Kolanda Douglas

Copyright © 2017 by Kolanda Douglas

All Rights Reserved. This book or any portion thereof may not be reproduced or used in any manner whatsoever without the express written permission of the publisher except for the use of brief quotations in a book review.

Printed in the United States of America

Titles are available at special discounts for bulk purchases by corporations, institutions, and other organizations.

www.kolandadouglas.com

Church Girls Just Want to Have Fun
Cover Designed by: Grey Scale Media Group Inc.

Library of Congress Control Number: TBD

ISBN: 978-0-9987375-0-8

Scripture quotations are taken from the *Holy Bible*, Amplified, King James Version, New King James, New Living Translation, New International Version, and The Message Versions.

Church Girls Just Want to Have Fun is a work of fiction. All characters and places appearing in this work are fictitious. Any resemblance to real persons, living or dead, places, establishments, events, organizations, and/or locations is purely coincidental and a product of the author's mind.

The scanning, uploading, and distribution of this book via the Internet or any other means without the permission of the publisher is illegal and punishable by law.

First Printing, 2017

For teenagers approaching the threshold of dating and their parents who anxiously wait for the nightmare to end

Acknowledgments

Church Girls Just Want to Have Fun is truly a labor of love. Every word, every detail, every chapter was written with you, the reader, in mind. I wrote to include the details and discussions I wanted to read in the countless fiction Christian novels I've read in the past about teenage dating. Therefore, this book is guaranteed to be authentic and familiar to the modern-day teenage Christian.

My storytelling approach on the matter is informal because teenage dating is a topic that can be categorized with death, estate planning and financial planning. Nobody wants to discuss it, everyone claims they will discuss it when necessary. However, by the time the discussion is needed, it's often too late. I intend to change the stigmas about teenage dating and provoke much needed discussion with *Church Girls Just Want to Have Fun*.

Although this story is loosely based on my experiences, I couldn't have written it with my strength alone. Lord, I'm forever grateful. Great is thy faithfulness! I'm in awe of what You have accomplished through me and I live in anticipation of the battles that will be won as a result.

To my village readers, your feedback and input is invaluable.

Daddy, Mommy and Tee, thank you for your roles in the story of my life and the time you sacrificed for the sake of this book.

To my son, Makai, thank you for pushing mommy into her calling. Before you arrived, I tiptoed around it but your arrival made me finally jump. You are my "why."

To my husband, Marcus, my best friend, and Superman, choosing to share your life with me wrote this book. Thank you for allowing me to share our story with the world. I love you.

Kolanda

PROLOGUE

"He can't be serious," Robyn thought rolling her eyes.

"What's wrong with James?" Jason asked.

"Nothing's wrong with him. I'm just not interested," Robyn answered.

For the last hour and a half, Jason lobbied for his best friend, James, trying to convince Robyn that she should get to know him because they would be great together.

Digging deeper, Jason replied, "You don't even know him. How do you know you're not interested?"

"I just know," Robyn quickly retorted.

Speaking sharply, "That's what's wrong with women today, y'all are so busy judging the cover you don't take the time to find out what's inside." Jason argued relentlessly.

"Please don't get me started on what's wrong with men today," Robyn said with an attitude.

"Okay," Jason surrendered. "You're right."

"Mm-hmm," Robyn said laughing.

"But seriously, my dude isn't like these other guys you know or you're use to," Jason continued, not taking no for an answer. "You know I wouldn't steer you wrong; I wouldn't do that to you."

"Yeah, I know."

"Besides, we all grew up in the same church," Jason pointed out. "Just like you and I have some things in common, I know you and James have some things in common too. Like, both of your birthdays are in September so you both started school late."

Intrigued, but not ready to give in just yet, Robyn asked, "Jason, does he know you're doing this?"

"Does it matter?" Jason wondered aloud, seeming slightly annoyed.

"Yes, it matters Jason. I don't want a guy that isn't mature or confident enough to approach me himself."

"Well, if you must know-,"

"Yes, I must," she interrupted.

"You're a trip," Jason jeered. "I hope James is ready."

Sucking her teeth, Robyn shouted jokingly, "Just tell me what was said."

Letting out a huge sigh, Jason said, "James and I were talking the other day and somehow the conversation got on you. Without giving you too many details, James basically mentioned he thought you were attractive and he wouldn't be opposed to getting to know you better."

"Then why didn't he call me himself?"

"Honestly?"

"Of course."

"He said you seemed unapproachable."

"Ouch."

"Yeah. So I just took it upon myself to play the middle man."

"Okay, another question."

"What now?" Jason asked, irritated.

"Last question, I promise."

Sensing Jason's frustration but unmoved by it, Robyn thought, *"So what if he's frustrated? He better be patient and answer all my questions if he wants me to do this."*

Pushing the limits, Robyn asked, "If James and I have attended the same church since we were babies and we've never been friends or even associates, don't you think that's a sign?"

8

"No," Jason answered firmly. "There's no harm in making a new friend. And if it happens to turn into something more, that should be a plus, right?"

Still not convinced, Robyn sighed, "I don't know. You know I'm the talkative, in-your-face, center-of-attention type. But James seems like the quiet, loner, laid-back type. I don't see how that's going to work."

"Stop making excuses and give it a chance," Jason huffed. "Hey, you never know."

Seeing that Jason wasn't going to let the subject go, Robyn conceded, "Okay, okay, I guess it won't hurt to at least talk to him."

Taking a slight pause, Robyn resumed, "If this blows up in my face and I get hurt, you and I will have a problem…a huge one."

"I know and trust me, I believe you," Jason laughed.

CHAPTER ONE

For I know the thoughts that I think toward you, saith the LORD, thoughts of peace, and not of evil, to give you an expected end. – Jeremiah 29:11 (KJV)

Six Months Later

Grateful to finally be home after a long day of school and cheerleading practice, Robyn was in the kitchen talking to her mom, Sharon, and younger sister, Renee, before excusing herself.

Walking into her pale blue-colored bedroom, she locked the door before plopping on the bed. School had been routine as usual but cheerleading practice had been exhausting with the regional competition coming up.

Monday practices were always tough coming off of the weekends.

Looking at the door again, Robyn relaxed. She remembered it was locked, she was safe. Reaching inside her pillowcase the picture slipped out onto her bed. Laying her head on her pillow, with dreamy, brown sparkling eyes, she stared at the picture of...James.

Pictured in his marching band uniform, James stood securely, smiling the shy little smile Robyn had grown to love. The sweet slip of the picture from him to her yesterday after church added an extra flair to her stride.

Holding the picture to her heart, Robyn wondered, *"Is this really happening? I've never liked a guy as much as I like James. I like everything about him, the way he walks, the way he talks, his confidence..."*

Pulling the picture away from her to study it closer, Robyn marveled, *"I guess Jason knew what he was doing after all because I especially like James' full, pink lips, his long eyelashes that spill over his rounded eyes, and the way his clothes fit perfectly on his tall, slender, caramel-colored frame. I don't know how I missed it before, James is fine."*

Despite his good looks, Robyn was happy James wasn't the yes-I'm-fine-and-I-know-it type of eighteen-year-old, he was modest in a way that made him all the more irresistible.

Reluctantly prying her eyes from the picture to check the clock on her desk, her cheeks blushed in anticipation. It was almost time for James to call.

Ever since Jason formally introduced them at church, they'd talked every night and always had a good time. They laughed at the same things, almost simultaneously, and finished each other's sentences. It felt as if they'd known each other for years. Their connection was undeniable.

Ring! Ring!

"On time, as usual," Robyn said to herself as she read 7:30 p.m. on the clock. She jumped up and snatched her cell phone off its charger.

"Hello?" She answered sweetly.

"I don't think I heard the phone ring on my end," James said laughing. "You must've been waiting to talk to me."

"Whatever," she replied laughing. "How do you know the phone didn't ring several times on this end?"

"Did it?"

"Maybe."

"Mm-hmm. It's cool. I really want to talk to you too."

"Oh yeah?" She blushed. "About what?"

"Everything."

Robyn loved his honesty. He was never shy about what he was feeling or thinking.

"But let's start with you telling me how your day went," James said, reeling her back into the conversation.

"It was good, just long. Cheerleading practice was hard as usual but I did well on my stunts so that's all that matters."

She didn't know whether he noticed but she never gave him a bad report about practice. She would never tell him about the number of times she didn't stick her stunts and fell out of the air.

"My girl," he stated matter-of-factly.

Smiling brightly, she asked, "How was your day?"

"It was cool."

"Just cool? That's it?"

"Yeah, it was okay," James answered again.

"Like that's any better," Robyn teased.

"I guess not," James agreed. "My day was weird. It felt like I was just going through the motions."

Wrinkling her forehead, she asked, "What's wrong?"

"Nothing's wrong, I just had a hard time concentrating today. I have a lot on my mind."

"Like what?" She was curious. She thought they talked about everything.

"I'm under a bit of pressure, that's all. Since it's my senior year, my parents are on me about finishing strong, band practice is getting longer and longer because graduation is coming up, and on top of all that, I have to make decisions about college. Time is winding down and I'm still not sure what school I what to attend, what major I want to pursue, or if I even want to attend college."

Understanding his dilemma, Robyn agreed, "Yeah, that's a lot of pressure." Gently approaching the subject, she asked, "So, what are you thinking?"

It was important for her to know his plans because they'd never talked about it. She'd assumed they hadn't discussed it because he had everything worked out, not because he didn't have a plan.

"See, that's the thing, I'm not exactly sure," he opened up, admitting his uncertainty. "My dad wants me to go to college and major in business and while my mom never gives her opinion, it's obvious she agrees with my dad. But a career in business just isn't me, I hate math. If I went that route, it would only be for the money. You know my passion is music. I enjoy playing the trumpet in the marching band and playing the organ at church. To me, playing those instruments are more than hobbies. I love doing it."

On the other end of the phone, Robyn remained quiet.

"Do you want to hear the truth?" James asked softly.

"Of course, what is it?"

"I think I want a career in music," James announced.

"If that's what you want, go for it!" Robyn replied.

James had been playing the organ at church for as long as she could remember. When he was eight years old, a popular organist came to play at their church for a concert. After the concert, the organist asked James to join him on the organ and showed him a few chords. After watching the organist's hands intently, James subsequently played what he'd heard and observed. That was the day he discovered his gift for music and from that moment on, he'd worked hard to improve his natural talent and abilities.

"That's easier said than done," James scoffed. "It's going to be tough convincing Eric and Diane Alexander their youngest wants to be a musician. Especially when their eldest son is an architect and their daughter is a pharmacist."

Robyn didn't know much about James' older brother and sister, Omar and Tiana, except what he'd told her. She knew throughout their childhood, Omar had been passionate about baseball and Tiana had been passionate about dance like James was about music. However, after high school, Omar and Tiana both traded in their passions for the corporate world. While they seemed to be happy, she wondered if they had any regrets.

Trying to find a bright side, Robyn suggested, "I don't know, your parents may surprise you."

"I doubt it."

Praying she wasn't overstepping her boundaries, Robyn questioned, "Then tell me, why would your father arrange for you to play at church if he didn't believe you played well enough to make it a career?"

Blowing out a huge sigh, James said, "Robyn, you don't know my father. He believes a man should work whether it's his passion or makes him happy. My father believes a man's responsibility is to provide."

Sitting up in her bed, Robyn offered, "I know everyone in the music business doesn't make it right away but with your talent, I'm sure music will eventually allow you to provide like you're supposed to."

In a defeated tone, James responded, "Keyword, eventually."

Sensing the discussion was coming to an end, Robyn encouraged, "Look, it's only February so you still have four months before graduation to decide, and then there's the summer. Promise me you won't stress about it too much, you should be enjoying your Senior year."

"You're right. I don't want to talk about it anymore," James responded abruptly.

"Okay," she replied coolly. "I'm here whenever you do."

"I know," he sighed. "Let's talk about something else."

"Okay. What's on your mind?"

"Us."

Robyn's stomach flipped. Sometimes his honesty was unnerving.

"Us?" She said to herself, but loud enough for James to hear.

"Yes, us. I've been thinking about us a lot too."

"What about us?"

"I know you've noticed our chemistry," James answered, getting straight to the point. "It's pretty hard to miss, it's so intense. I want more. I'm tired of just being your friend."

Unsure of how to respond, Robyn simply said his name, "James."

They had never talked about the electric current that sparked and caught fire between them from day one. They had always ignored it, until now.

"No," he said, silencing her. "Let me finish, I need to say this," he sighed. "Robyn, I have never met a girl like you and I've never liked anyone as much as I like you. You aren't like most seventeen-year-old girls I know. I think growing up in church has made you different from the rest. You have this unexplainable confidence, it's so attractive."

Squeezing her eyes shut to block out her horrifying past, Robyn cupped her face with her hands and thought, *"If you only knew."*

"You could have any guy you want but you don't waste your time with just anybody; and I like that about you, it makes me feel special." James replied.

Feeling the heat rising in her cheeks, Robyn felt she was about to melt so she tried again by saying his name, "James."

Ignoring her, yet again, James continued, "That confidence is even shown in the way you carry yourself. You are so beautiful. I've always been captivated by your round face, dark brown eyes, flat nose, and thin pink lips even before we started talking. And as if those features weren't beautiful enough, they work together to create the ideal backdrop for your best feature- your smile."

Robyn sighed loudly, deciding it was better to just wait until the sweet agony ended before she tried to speak again.

"Robyn, are you still there?" James asked after a moment.

"Yes," she whispered, finally able to utter something other than his name.

"Promise me something."

"Anything," she breathed.

"If we do this and it doesn't work out the way we hoped, promise me we can still be friends. I don't want to lose your friendship, it means too much."

"I-I promise," she stammered.

"Good."

Robyn was speechless. Her thoughts were all over the place. She could barely form sentences. She spent the next hour on the phone responding to James with "Mm-hmm" and "Oh yeah."

When she didn't think she could get away with half-listening anymore, she reminded him she had homework to finish.

"Okay, I'll talk to you tomorrow," he said. "Don't stay up too late, I want my girlfriend looking good at school tomorrow."

Robyn's insides squealed, she thought, *"Girlfriend?!"* It was the first time he'd said the word and she loved the way it rolled off his tongue.

"Yes sir," she uttered with a small voice.

"That's my girl."

Trying to regain control of her emotions, Robyn beamed saying, "James?"

"Yeah?"

Now from the position of girlfriend, she had one last thing to say, "Don't let your parents' plans for your life overshadow yours. You can do anything you put your mind to accomplish. You're responsible for the life of James Alexander, not them. Okay?"

James let out a loud sigh. "Thanks, I really needed to hear that," he paused. "See? This is why I upgraded your position," he laughed.

"Shut up," Robyn laughed. "I'm glad I could help. I hope you have a great day tomorrow. Goodnight."

"Goodnight. Sweet dreams."

Robyn bit her lip to keep from smiling as she reluctantly ended the call.

"Wow, I have a boyfriend."

The smile she'd tried to hold back, resurfaced. This time she gave in to it.

"I actually have a boyfriend," she said again, hugging her pillow and jumping on the bed.

CHAPTER TWO

Let them alone and disregard them; they are blind guides and teachers. And if a blind man leads a blind man, both will fall into a ditch. – Matthew 15:14 (AMP)

Beep-beep-beep! Beep-beep-beep! Beep-beep-beep!

The constant blaring of the alarm clock signaled a new day as Robyn stirred in her bed. With chirping birds outside her window and the sun shining brightly through the blinds, it was indeed morning.

Groaning as she reached to turn the alarm off, she whispered, "It's too soon."

She felt like she hadn't slept all night. Her mind had been filled with vivid dreams of James. She dreamt about their first date, their first kiss, prom, and how her friends would react when they found out she had a boyfriend. Most of all, her thoughts had been filled with how she was going to tell her parents she had a boyfriend.

"Ugh, mommy and daddy," she grunted, pulling the covers over her head.

Bursting into Robyn's bedroom from their adjoining bathroom, Renee exclaimed, "What's wrong?"

"Nothing," Robyn quickly replied, sitting up.

"But you called for mom and dad." Renee pointed out.

"Yeah but it's nothing," she retorted, trying to convince Renee with a smile.

"Okay, if you say so," Renee replied hesitantly, closing the door.

Robyn had no idea how she would tell her parents about James. But she knew she had to at least tell her mom, and fast. Her mother had a sixth sense when it came to her daughters; she never missed a beat with them. She just hoped her mother wouldn't be too disappointed she hadn't shared her true feelings about James all along.

19

Although her parents knew she and James had become friends, they had no idea about the connection they shared. And while her mother had worked hard to ensure she and Renee could talk to her about anything, Robyn had been too embarrassed to confess her true feelings. She feared her mom would tell her she was either too young, moving too fast, or worst, that she was only feeling this way because James was the first guy she'd ever really liked. No matter the outcome, Robyn knew she needed to talk to her parents.

"James is important to me and telling them only shows how important. They'll respect that, right?" She asked herself. *"We attend the same church so it's not like I can actually hide it from them even if I wanted to."*

Looking at the clock on her nightstand, Robyn realized she only had thirty minutes to get ready for school. Crawling out of bed, she slowly headed to the bathroom to start her morning routine.

"You sure you're alright?" Renee asked, sticking her head in the door.

Picking up her toothbrush, Robyn looked at her sister, "I just need to talk to mom about something, that's all."

"Whatever it is, you better do it fast, you know how she is," Renee warned.

Putting toothpaste on her toothbrush, Robyn said, "Trust me, I know. I've been caught off guard too many times in the past to not be mindful of her intuition. It's like she knows everything."

Grumbling, Renee said, "Well, I hope it keeps her attention for a while. That way, she can leave me alone about cleaning my room."

Chuckling, Robyn spoke with a mouthful of toothpaste, "Wishful thinking."

"I guess so." Renee sighed, leaving.

Robyn wasn't sure how she would approach the subject. This would be the first time she'd ever talked to her mom about dating and she wanted to be taken seriously. She wanted her mom to see her as a young woman, not her daughter or a teenager.

Washing her face, Robyn said to herself, "I'll just have to avoid her this morning. Yeah, that's what I'm going to do- avoid her."

Back inside her bedroom, Robyn walked to her closet. Wanting to look especially nice for school on this special day, the day she would announce to her friends she had a boyfriend.

"Now that I've figured out how to handle mommy for the moment, I need to figure out my outfit for today. What am I going to wear?" She asked herself.

The winning outfit matched her heightened self-esteem and joy. Robyn donned a gray and white striped shirt with pink flowers that paired well with her favorite gray skinny jeans. She completed the outfit with silver, sparkly sandals to show her matching polished pink toes.

Looking into the mirror over her dresser, she pulled her straightened, black hair into a high ponytail and let the mane fall against her neck. However, the look wasn't complete until she put on her favorite silver bracelet and matching earrings.

Walking to the bedroom door, Robyn assessed her look in the full-length mirror her father nailed to the back of the door years ago.

What had been written by her mother as a reminder during her middle school years had become a daily affirmation. She read the post on the mirror aloud, "I am fearfully and wonderfully made."

For a brief moment, Robyn thought back to her first day of sixth grade and shuddered. She remembered it like it was yesterday.

One morning, five years ago, her parents received a call from the private school they wanted Robyn to attend. She'd been accepted and would be able to start that morning. After completing the required paperwork in the front office, her mother walked her to the door of her new classroom. "Have a wonderful day," her mother said and kissed her cheek. Robyn took a deep breath and went inside. Although the teacher, Ms. Rice, was at the chalkboard teaching, everyone turned their attention toward the door as Robyn entered the classroom.

"Who's that? She's cute!" One boy yelled out.

"Yeah, she is," another boy agreed.

"I like her hair," one girl said.

"And those earrings," another girl responded.

"Boys and girls, this is Robyn Cooley," Ms. Rice announced. "She will be joining our sixth-grade class so please make her feel welcome."

"Yes, Ms. Rice," the class answered in unison.

Robyn was so overwhelmed with her classmates' approving looks and comments, she did the one thing she did often- she smiled.

"Whoa! Your teeth look like they're doing the tootsie roll!" Someone yelled out.

The class laughed.

"Yeah, they look dangerous!" Another agreed.

The class continued to laugh.

Robyn stopped smiling, blood rushed to her cheeks, displaying her embarrassment. She was mortified.

Seeing this, Ms. Rice tried to regain the class' attention and chastise them at the same time. "Boys and girls, please remember the Golden Rule. Let's treat others the way we want to be treated."

"Robyn, I'm sorry," Ms. Rice continued. "Please sit at any available desk. I'll review today's lesson with you once the others get started on the classwork."

Robyn walked quietly to an available desk in the back and sunk in the chair. She had never been so humiliated or felt so low. Of course, she knew her two front teeth were crooked, they'd been that way since they grew in. But no one had ever taunted her about it so she never thought of it as a flaw. Experiencing it for the first time made her feel small. Unfortunately, Robyn went on to feel this way until the end of seventh grade.

After that first day in sixth grade, Robyn did things she wasn't proud of to prevent the teasing. She'd started hanging around the "cool kids," presenting behavioral problems in class, and allowing her grades to drop dramatically. She thought joining the in-crowd would make the others leave her alone. Sometimes it worked, other days it didn't. As a result, her emotions and self-esteem were in constant limbo.

Thankfully, the summer before eighth grade she got braces and they were removed before she started high school at a new school. Since then, Robyn promised herself she would never let someone else's opinion of her affect her behavior or how she felt about herself.

Renee's yelling snapped Robyn back into reality. "Robyn! Daddy's ready!"

Taking another glance in the mirror, Robyn yelled back, "I'm coming!" Grabbing her book bag from her closet, she sighed loudly, "Thank God that part of my life is over."

Inside of the garage, her father and sister were already waiting in the truck.

"Good morning Pookie," her father said, using the nickname he'd given her as a baby. "You almost got left."

"Sorry daddy, I lost track of time."

"No problem," he smiled.

"Where's mom?" Robyn asked carefully. "I didn't see her this morning."

"She left a little early, she has an early meeting this morning," her dad said, turning up the radio as his favorite gospel quartet sang through the speakers.

Satisfied, Robyn looked at her father and smiled. Walter Cooley was a no nonsense type of man who did not play about his wife, his daughters or his money. Though he was gentle and soft-spoken, he always spoke with authority. He believed in the power of prayer and hard work and consequently, he'd always been privileged to provide the best for his family.

Robyn closed her eyes and thanked God for her father. She had several friends with absent fathers; she did not take hers for granted. She made sure he knew how much she loved and appreciated him. He was an excellent husband and father.

Smiling, Robyn thought, "*No wonder mommy is so crazy about him.*"

"What are you smiling about?" Her dad asked, looking through the rearview mirror, his eyes twinkling.

"Just thinking," she answered, turning to face the window.

"She's been acting weird all morning." Robyn heard Renee say as she drifted back to her own thoughts.

Her parents had been married for twenty-five years.

Cringing, Robyn recalled the early years of her parents' marriage. She'd watched from the sidelines as her mother struggled to love, trust, and submit to her father because he did not share her fervor for Christ.

The spiritual imbalance was so overwhelming it affected their parenting. Her father missed many milestones and other significant moments in his daughters' lives due to a blurred focus. Consequently, her mother had appeared to others as a single parent.

Five years ago, Robyn noticed a change in her father. He initiated more family time, worked fewer hours and holidays, and began attending church regularly. She'd never learned what triggered the change but her mother's eyes had never shined brighter.

"Pookie!" Her father shouted, interrupting Robyn from her thoughts again.

"Yes sir?"

"We're at school," Renee chimed in, frowning. "Get out the truck. What's up with you today?"

"Sorry," Robyn smiled sheepishly. Sometimes she forgot how close they lived to their school.

"Have a wonderful day, girls. Love y'all." Her father beamed.

"Love you too daddy!" They sang in harmony, kissing his cheek.

Robyn opened the door and joined her sister on the sidewalk. Her father waved before driving away.

No longer able to keep the news to herself, Robyn blurted out, "James asked me to be his girlfriend last night!"

Crossing her arms across her chest, Renee replied, "Uh-huh, so that's why you're so weird this morning. So, what did you say?"

Looking down at her feet, Robyn slowly answered, "I said yes."

"Wow, your first boyfriend," Renee replied with shock. "I didn't realize y'all were that serious. Are you sure you're ready for this?"

Although Renee was nearly two years younger, she was much wiser when it came to matters of the heart. Robyn looked at her sister shrugging and said, "I think so. I admit I'm not sure what to expect and I'm a little nervous but this relationship isn't superficial. It's not about looks and personality alone either. We've spent a lot of time getting to know each other and we've clicked since the beginning."

Waiting for her sister to respond, Robyn looked away. She hoped she didn't sound pathetic.

Offering a smile of approval, Renee said, "Robyn, I know you. I know you would only date a guy if he was worth it so James must be great. If you're happy, then I'm happy for you."

"Really?!" Robyn shrieked. "You don't know how much that means to me," she said, pulling her sister into a bear hug.

"Let me go," Renee whined.

"Oh be quiet, you love it," she squeezed harder.

"No I don't," Renee teased, pulling herself out of the embrace. "I need to go; I have to talk to my teacher before class."

"Okay, I'll see you later," Robyn said, watching Renee walk toward the tenth-grade building.

"I'm so glad that went well!" Robyn rejoiced. *"Now, if only she could help me with mommy and daddy."*

Robyn walked in the opposite direction toward the eleventh-grade building. As she neared, she saw her best friend, Tanisha, talking to herself as she angrily snatched books from her book bag and hurled them in her locker.

"Oh Lord, what now?" Robyn thought, hurrying to her friend's side.

"Tee?" Robyn called, using her friend's nickname as she approached her with caution. "What's wrong?"

Tanisha looked at Robyn with tears in her eyes, "It happened again," she said, before weeping silently on Robyn's shoulder.

Robyn remained silent and held her friend. Though Tanisha hadn't said much, Robyn knew what she meant. Greg had cheated on her…again.

Greg was Tanisha's first real boyfriend. At seventeen, Tanisha had the body of a mature woman. And because of her curvaceous body, she received a lot of male attention. She had her pick of the litter; she could have anybody she wanted. Yet, she chose Greg and she'd never dated a guy longer than three months, until now.

Tanisha grew up without a father because he never wanted children. As a result, she had zero confidence in men. She didn't trust they would stick around so she ended the relationship before she was in too deep, emotionally. Three months was just enough time to give her the male attention she desired without the guy expecting too much from her, physically.

This method had worked for her until she met Greg.

Their relationship started off like any other relationship Tanisha had before. They went on dates, talked on the phone, and hung out with each other's friends. However, as the three-month mark came to an end, Tanisha wasn't ready to end it. She was too intrigued. Greg had only touched her when they hugged or held hands, kissed her forehead, he never mentioned sex, and their conversations were quite sophisticated. He seemed different. He seemed like the perfect gentleman so Tanisha continued to date him despite her three-month rule.

Once they entered the first week of their fourth month together, Tanisha lost her virginity.

That was two months ago and now, Greg had been caught cheating for the fourth time.

"Tee," Robyn said pulling her friend off her shoulder so she could look into her eyes. "You've got to leave Greg alone. How much longer are you going to let him do this to you?"

Shrugging her shoulders, Tanisha muttered, "I can't leave him, I love him."

Robyn knew Tanisha loved Greg. She would think Tanisha was strange if she didn't love Greg after he took her virginity. However, she was tired of Tanisha allowing Greg to take advantage of her. Ever since she started having sex with Greg, Tanisha wasn't the same loving, friendly, funny and confident person Robyn had known since ninth grade. She'd allowed Greg's heartless behavior change her. She'd become silly, insecure and sad.

Sighing deeply, Robyn softened her tone, "I know you love him but Tee, you should love yourself more."

"I know," Tanisha said in between sobs. "I'm trying."

———

Robyn's first and second period classes flew by. Both teachers used the entire period to review the last exam. She couldn't remember what happened in third period because she'd been too busy wondering what James was doing and how his day was going. She hoped he wasn't allowing the pressure from his parents to ruin another day.

During fourth period, while the rest of the class watched a movie, Robyn thought about how she would tell her friends about James. She couldn't decide if she wanted to tell them as soon as they sat down for lunch so it was all they talked about or if she'd tell them near the end of lunch so they couldn't ask too many questions. No matter how the conversation began, she knew they would be excited when they found out.

"Okay class, that's it for today," Mr. Hughes, her history teacher, announced. "For homework, I want you to read pages 210-233. There may or may not be a pop quiz tomorrow."

"Ugh," Robyn groaned, gathering her belongings, hurrying to her locker.

"Robyn!"

She turned around as her friend Jasmine ran toward her.

"Hey, we're staying on campus today for lunch. Let's go grab a table so we don't have to eat outside," Jasmine said, pulling Robyn away from her locker.

The cafeteria was already packed with hungry upperclassmen. Robyn grabbed the last available table big enough to seat their crew just as a group of freshman girls were about to sit down.

"Sorry ladies," Jasmine said sarcastically.

Shaking her head, Robyn laughed, "You are so mean."

"Whaaaat?" Jasmine asked batting her eyes, trying her best to look innocent.

"Robyn! Jasmine!"

The girls looked up as their friend Olivia walked toward them with their other friends, Erin, Tanisha, and Jelena in tow. They greeted each other then grabbed their lunch in pairs, to secure their table, before they all settled down to eat.

The table conservation began as usual. Robyn listened as the girls talked about their classes and the latest drama in Greg and Tanisha's relationship. When it seemed like there were no other pressing matters to discuss, Robyn decided to make her move.

"Sooo ladies," Robyn began, clearing her throat. "I have an announcement to make."

"Okay," Tanisha said with a puzzled look on her face.

Robyn knew Tanisha was trying to figure out what she had to announce to the group that she hadn't told her first. Ignoring the look, Robyn took a deep breath and said, "I have a boyfriend."

No one said a word, they stared blankly at Robyn.

"Did y'all hear what I said? I said, I have a boyfriend," Robyn repeated with excitement.

"We heard you," Jelena spoke first. "I think we're all in shock. We just can't believe little Miss Priss actually has a boyfriend. I mean, you're so picky, we honestly thought you'd never get a boyfriend."

"What?" Robyn asked.

"What she means," Erin chimed in, "Is that your standards are so high we didn't think any guy would be good enough to meet them. But, we're glad someone did, right girls?"

Although they all nodded their heads in agreement, Robyn didn't believe the smiles plastered across their faces. She was shocked by their response and not to mention, a little offended.

"Oh, so y'all sit and talk about me when I'm not around?" She asked, raising her voice.

"No. It's not like that," Tanisha interjected.

"Well, I don't think I'm picky," Robyn said matter-of-factly, trying to regain her composure. "I just know what I want and I'm not willing to settle because I know-"

"Ugh, here she goes," Jelena sucked her teeth.

"What do you mean, here she goes?" Robyn scoffed, rolling her eyes.

"What I mean is-," Jelena began.

"She meant nothing by that," Tanisha jumped in, taking control of the conversation. "So, who is he? What's he like? Where did y'all meet? And why didn't I know you were talking to someone," she asked, looking disappointed.

"I know Tee," Robyn replied, seeing Tanisha's eyes. "I didn't want to say anything because I wasn't sure where it would lead. It's not because I didn't want you to know," she said, hoping Tanisha would understand.

"So, what's his name?" Tanisha asked again, signaling she did understand.

"His name is James Alexander," Robyn answered.

"Oh, that's a strong name. He sounds rich!" Olivia said with excitement.

Robyn laughed. "No, he's not rich but he is caring, he's a musician, and such a gentleman," she boasted. "We met at church. We've been going to the same church since we were babies." She smiled to herself as she remembered how she'd never cared for James as a child.

"Church?" Jelena asked with a laugh while Olivia, Jasmine, and Erin did their best to stifle their giggles. "This just keeps getting better and better."

"Yes, church. What's wrong with that?" Robyn asked.

"Nothing's wrong with it," Jasmine said. "But where are y'all gonna go on dates? Sunday School and Bible Study?" She asked sarcastically.

"That might be fun," Erin said dryly.

Robyn didn't respond, she just stared at them. She didn't want to dignify their immaturity with a response.

"Robyn," Tanisha called softly. "What I think they're trying to say is, how much fun can you have with a "church boy?" Your first boyfriend should be someone who can show you a good time, someone you can create new experiences with. But if your first boyfriend is a "church boy," he might be too holy to do anything."

"James isn't like that," Robyn said. "We grew up in church, not a cult."

"Robyn, you may not want to hear it but Tee's right," Olivia said. "Besides, good boys aren't fun."

The girls nodded in agreement.

"That's not true," Robyn mumbled, sitting back in her chair to eat the rest of her lunch in silence, while her thoughts rang loudly, *"I thought a good guy was what every woman hoped for. A good guy is the perfect first boyfriend."*

Robyn couldn't believe the girls' reactions. It was the complete opposite of what she'd imagined.

CHAPTER THREE

A gentle answer deflects anger, but harsh words make tempers flare.
– Proverbs 15:1 (NLT)

Robyn closed her bedroom door sinking to the floor. Closing her eyes, she wanted to stop the recurring memory of the lunch fiasco.

"There's no way I can date the kind of guys they like and expect different results; I would have the same issues." Robyn said aloud.

If possible, Robyn wanted to avoid dating experiences that involved heart break, cheating, lying, and being treated like anything less than a princess. She'd decided the only way to avoid those experiences was to date someone different and she really believed she'd accomplished that with James.

Knock. Knock.

"Come in," Robyn answered, moving away from the door.

"How did it go today?" Renee asked, sitting on Robyn's bed.

"How did what go?" She asked, confused.

"I know you told your friends about James." Renee smiled. "You know you can't keep a secret."

Robyn tried to smile back. "I wish I could keep a secret."

"What happened?" Renee asked.

Robyn couldn't keep much from Renee. Her smile or the lack thereof always told Renee when she needed to talk.

"They didn't react the way I'd hoped," Robyn said. "Instead of being happy I'd finally found someone who met my standards, they told me he wasn't good enough."

Frowning, Renee asked, "What? James is a good guy."

"I know!" Robyn blushed. "I just wish the girls could see that. But, no. They think my first boyfriend shouldn't be so conservative. They think

33

our relationship will be dull because he's a "church boy." They think I should date guys more like their type, like Greg," she scoffed, pretending to puke.

"That's crazy!" Renee shouted. "Greg is a dog and conservative or not, James is still a man-"

"Yes, he is," Robyn purred.

"Girl, please," Renee said shaking her head. "Anyway, don't let them discourage you from doing what you want to do. They're probably jealous they haven't found a guy like James and won't admit it."

"Mmm."

"Think about it, you're doing something different. Some people see that as you thinking you're too good to be like them."

"Wow." Robyn stared at her sister in disbelief. "Sometimes I wonder if you're really the older sister."

Renee smiled. "Just keep your relationship to yourself," she suggested.

"I just don't understand why they don't see this as an opportunity for them to follow my lead and date guys who are different too."

"Do you hear yourself?"

"Yes, I think what I said makes sense."

"Don't get me wrong, it does make sense. It makes sense to us. However, you're asking the majority in this situation to follow the lead of the minority, which, in this case, is you."

"Seems like common sense to me," Robyn said, shrugging her shoulders.

"I agree," Renee reassured. "But obviously, everybody doesn't think like that. So, don't tell them everything. That only gives them ammunition to hurt you."

"You're right. I don't know why their approval means so much to me," she said sadly. "But that's not the worst part. I couldn't even count on Tanisha for support; she was practically leading the pack."

"Can you blame her?" Renee asked.

"I'm not sure I know what you mean," Robyn answered, confused.

"Look at her situation," Renee continued. "She's in love with a guy who doesn't love or respect her and here you are talking about your guy who respects you, has good values, and goes to church. She's jealous!"

"Jealous?" She frowned. "No," she said, shaking her head. "Tee and I have been friends too long for her to be jealous. It's not like I was intentionally trying to hurt her feelings by telling her about James. I really thought she'd be happy for me."

"Y'all may be friends but she's still human. I'm sure she doesn't think you were trying to hurt her but she's probably jealous that your first boyfriend isn't likely to treat you the same way Greg treats her," Renee explained. "Tell me, what do people usually do when they're jealous of you?"

"They either try to tear you down or discourage you," Robyn answered sadly.

"Exactly."

Renee continued talking but Robyn didn't hear another word. She was still trying to process her sister's revelation about her best friend.

———

Robyn pressed ignore on the phone again. Tanisha was calling for the third time but Robyn wasn't ready to talk to her. She didn't know what to say to her, she was still upset. Afraid she may say the wrong thing, she'd decided to avoid Tanisha altogether until she'd figured out what to say.

35

Ring! Ring!

"Doesn't she get it?" Robyn huffed, flipping the phone over, ready to press ignore again.

It was James.

"Hi James," she whispered into the phone.

"Hey girl," James responded. "I can't talk long tonight, I need to study for a math test. I need to score at least a "C" to keep my dad off my back."

Serving him with a huge sigh, Robyn responded, "Okay."

James chuckled. "You do want me to pass the test don't you?"

"Of course, I was just looking forward to the distraction."

"Oh no," he exhaled. "I was hoping your day was better than mine."

"I doubt it."

"Really? I was looking forward to hearing about your day; I need something to make me smile."

"Well, I'm sorry to disappoint," she sulked.

"Trust me, you are not a disappointment."

"Thanks," she grinned, alleviating some of her tension.

"So, tell me. What happened?"

"I had a conversation with my friends today and they didn't respond the way I thought they would. I thought they would be excited about my news but their response made me feel like they don't even know me."

"Well, what's the news? Maybe I can help you figure out why they responded the way they did."

"I'm not telling you," she laughed nervously, "It's girl talk."

"Oh, it must have been about me." He concluded.

"If you think so," she replied, trying her best to sound indifferent.

"Yes, I do think so and I'm flattered."

Robyn rolled her eyes; she could hear the smirk in his voice.

"Now back to your day," he paused. "I think you're taking these friendships too seriously."

"I don't know how else to take them."

"I mean," James hesitated, "You should take your friendships seriously in the sense they should be able to trust you and you should be able to trust them. However, you shouldn't take them so seriously you think you'll be best friends forever. I hate to say it but if you think they don't understand you now, chances are they probably won't understand you in the future either."

"I'd hate to think of my friendships that way," Robyn grimaced. "Besides, I like happy endings so I hope they last forever."

"For your sake, I hope they do too."

Robyn smiled.

"I'm just saying," James continued, "You still have a lot of maturing to do and the qualities you need in a friend now may not be the qualities you need in a friend later, just be careful."

"Okay, I see what you're saying. I'll just hope for the best and be more conscience."

"That's fine; I just don't want to see you upset about friendships that may not last past high school."

"Thanks for caring James."

"Of course. Also, you think they know you but they really may not know you. I told you yesterday that you're different."

"You know, this is the second time I've heard that today."

"Well, whoever said it must be wise too."

"Oh, I'm sure Renee would love to hear that, so, tell me, how am I different?"

"Uh, let's see. Before you experience something, you'd rather get advice from someone who's already been through it."

"Right."

"Most people would rather blaze their own trail and make their own mistakes."

"That's crazy."

"Ouch," James replied. "I feel like that's what I'm doing when it comes to music. Instead of following my parents' recipe for success, I want to create my own."

"See, that's different," she said, hoping James understood that she wasn't trying to offend him. "I'm talking about people who go through situations where there's a general outcome. Like my friend who's dating a guy she knows is cheating on her but she's hoping one day she'll be enough for him. I mean, come on, everybody knows in this type of situation, the man never commits or changes as long as the woman tolerates his behavior."

"So, I bet you're the envy of all your friends now, huh?"

"What do you mean?"

"Well, because I would never do that to you."

Yet again James' comment caught her off guard and she couldn't think of anything to say. Even over the phone, he had a way of making her go from confident to bashful. Turning a shade of deep red, Robyn thought, *"Whoa. Okay then, he's already committed to not cheating on me. It just confirms that he really is something special."*

"You know we're never going to finish a conversation if you stop and blush at everything I say," James teased.

38

"Who says I'm blushing?"

"I know you are."

"You think you know me huh?"

"I don't have to think, I know I know you."

"Mm-hmm so anyway," she replied, wanting to change the subject, "How was your day?"

"Don't try to change the subject."

"What?" She feigned innocence. "You've helped me so now I want to hear about your day," she said, trying to sound genuine.

"Yeah, okay," James replied with sarcasm.

"Again," she said, still trying to regain her composure, "How was your day?"

"It was cool until band practice."

"What happened?"

"Forget it, it's embarrassing."

"It can't be that bad."

"Trust me, it is."

"Okay," she paused. "What if I tell you something embarrassing about me? Then, will you tell me what happened?"

"You? Embarrassed? I don't believe it."

"Oh trust me, I get embarrassed," she assured.

"But you're so confident, so forward. Doesn't that kind of eliminate the chances of embarrassment?"

"Not at all."

"Well, this I've got to hear."

"Okay, I'll go first then you're next," she paused, waiting for his answer.

"Deal," he agreed after a moment.

"Here it goes," she sighed. "One Tuesday night, my mom, Renee and I were at church for rehearsal for the Christmas play. I was already annoyed that my mom was helping with the play because that meant Renee and I had to participate."

"Wait, how old were you?"

"That's not important, this story is embarrassing enough."

"This must've been recent." He sneered.

"And for whatever reason," Robyn continued, ignoring his comment, "I became more and more annoyed the longer we were there. I started complaining about being there, the cast, the costumes, everything. After a while, my mom told me to stop complaining because she was tired of hearing it but I kept going."

"No, you didn't," James gasped.

"Yes. I didn't think she would do anything crazy in front of everyone, boy was I was wrong," Robyn shuddered. "Before I realized what was happening, she'd grabbed me by the collar in front of everyone warning me to stop trying her; I was so embarrassed."

"Wow," James said, obviously stunned. "I can't see your mom doing that."

"Learn from me," Robyn advised, "Don't ever underestimate her gentleness. She does not play."

"I don't know what to say," he laughed. "What happened in band practice wasn't that bad. I just let someone get the best of me so I acted out of character, that's all," James said hurriedly.

Embarrassed all over again. She'd told him an embarrassing story for nothing. "No sir, I don't think so; I need more details. You're not getting off that easily after what I just shared."

James huffed. "I was leaving seventh period when I ran into Shawn."

"Who is Shawn?"

James had never mentioned anyone named Shawn before.

"He's one of the trumpet players in the band."

"Oh, you've never mentioned him before," Robyn decided to say.

"We don't really talk outside of band. But today he comes up to me and says, "Hey man, let's head to practice." I was a little caught off guard but I told him I was skipping practice to study for a math test. So, he looks at me with the stupidest grin and says, "I understand, do what you have to do. I'll hold down the section for you.""

"Uh-oh."

"I ignored the comment," James replied. "I told him to let me know how things go and walked away. Then, I started thinking, what if he's actually better than me?"

"Impossible."

"I wish I had your confidence. I put off studying for band practice because I wanted to be sure Shawn wasn't given the chance to show he was better than me. Then, I ended up embarrassing myself because he and I were competing during practice the entire time. The band director called us out several times."

"Competing?"

"Yeah, we were trying to outplay each other which made it difficult for the rest of the section to be heard."

"They probably thought you'd lost it," Robyn chuckled.

"I'm sure. It was pathetic."

"That's not like you but I understand why you did it."

"You do?"

Giggling, she pointed out, "He challenged you and it bruised your little ego."

"I can't even lie, you saw right through that," he laughed too. "I'm usually modest about my gift. I don't know why I let Shawn get the best of me."

"I think this thing with your parents about your future is affecting you more than you think."

Jame didn't reply.

"Every time you argue with your parents, it's like they're challenging your ability but you can't really squash that fight without being disrespectful."

"True."

"Now, here comes someone else trying to challenge you so you decided to squash it…well, you tried," Robyn joked.

"Oh, I squashed it," James assured. "I probably looked crazy while doing it but it's squashed. Believe that."

Shaking her head, Robyn replied, "Men, always competing with each other."

"You think you know me, huh?" James asked.

"What did you say earlier? I don't have to think, I know I know you."

"Well, if band practice was any indication of what it would be like to fight my parents on what I should do after graduation, I should just do what they want. Tonight was draining."

"No," Robyn stated firmly. "You can't compare this to the disagreement about your future. It's completely different."

"I wish you were around during the conversations with my parents, you always know what to say."

"Unfortunately, you've got to handle that on your own."

"I know-" James grunted. "Hold on a minute." She heard him put the phone down. He was talking to someone.

"Robyn?"

"I'm still here," she answered.

"Let me call you back; my mom is at the door."

"Okay, talk to you later. I hope your night turns around."

"Me too," James said before hanging up.

Settling into the chair at her desk, Robyn sighed, "I need to follow my own advice. I'm encouraging James to talk to his parents about something hard, it's time to figure out how I'm going to talk to mommy."

CHAPTER FOUR

May He grant you your heart's desire and fulfill all your plans.
– Psalm 20:4 (AMP)

If the family dinner she'd just experienced was any indication of what she would face, the longer she put off telling her parents about James, Robyn knew, she needed to talk to her mom right away.

Robyn hadn't enjoyed the meal or the conversation because she'd been too distracted with monitoring herself. She'd clearly eaten out of habit because she couldn't remember what her mom cooked or how it tasted. All of her senses had been zeroed in on her tone, her demeanor, her level of interaction, and whether she was being too chatty or not chatty enough. She didn't want her mother to suspect anything.

"I want to show mommy that I've really thought about this so I need to anticipate what she may say or ask," Robyn reasoned aloud. "Plus, I need to have a strong argument just in case I start losing her."

She didn't expect a heated discussion because she planned to talk to her mother alone. She was not going to talk to her father about this. No doubt he would flip out. She would let her mom be responsible for letting her dad know.

Even if her mom sensed what was going on before she had a chance to initiate the conversation, she wanted to be prepared. Grabbing a notebook and pen from her backpack, Robyn wrote two questions she was sure her mom would ask when we talk and the explanations she would provide.

Why do I want a boyfriend?

I want a boyfriend because I want a boy that's also a close friend. A boyfriend is a different kind of friend. This will be a friend that I deeply care about and who deeply cares about me. I want James as my boyfriend because he cares about me, my family, my school work, my grades, and my relationship with Christ. Not only that, he knows and respects my parents.

Why do I need a boyfriend?

I need to begin identifying the qualities I want in a husband. I have to tell God what I want in a husband so He can begin training that special man made just for me. Who knows? This guy could be the one that I'm supposed to marry.

Satisfied with her explanations, Robyn decided to create a pros and cons list about dating James. "It can't hurt to be overly prepared," she assured herself. "I hope this shows mommy my level of maturity, how serious I consider this topic, and what I'm willing to do to have James as my boyfriend."

PROS

- ✓ He has goals
- ✓ He's a gentleman
- ✓ Mom knows and likes him, she can help with dad
- ✓ We developed a friendship first
- ✓ Someone, other than family, cares about me

46

✓ We're always at church; we both participate in church

✓ He encourages me to do my best in school

✓ We have the same religion and share similar beliefs

✓ I believe God is happy with this because we're both Christian teenagers

✓ We've discussed God and the Bible on the phone. Mom always says, if you can't talk about God with him you don't need to be with him

✓ He respects the rules of the house. He respects my 10 p.m. phone curfew; we hang up at least five minutes before curfew

✓ We share the same feelings about premarital sex (*we both want to wait until marriage to have sex*)

CONS

X Peer pressure

X If it doesn't work, I'll lose a friend

X In the heat of the moment, can we trust ourselves?

X My grades aren't as well as I'd like. Do I have time to better my grades and have a boyfriend?

X Am I ready for what a relationship involves?

X Is he really different? I mean, he is still a man

"That should do it." Robyn smiled, pleased with herself. She was especially grateful to discover the pros outweighed the cons. That fact alone multiplied her confidence.

"Robyn!" Her mother called. "Come here please!"

Walking into the family room, Robyn found her parents cuddled on the couch watching TV.

"Ma'am?"

"Honey, look!" Her mother said, pointing at Robyn. "I told you," she said to her husband.

Robyn's father turned to look at her. "I don't see it," he replied, turning his attention back to the TV.

"See what?" Robyn asked, frowning.

"You know I know when something is going on with my girls," her mother replied. "What's up?" She asked, sitting up.

"How does she do that?!" Robyn let out a deep sigh. "What makes you think something is up?" She asked, innocently.

"Your behavior during dinner," her mother replied. "You were sitting at the table but I could tell your mind was somewhere else."

"Shoot, I knew I overdid it." Robyn scolded herself.

"Tell me, what's going on?" Her mother asked again.

"I really wanted to wait for a better time to talk about it," Robyn said hesitantly. *"Plus I need my notes"!"* She shrieked inwardly.

"What's wrong with right now?" Her mother asked.

"Nothing," she exhaled.

"Let's hear it then." Her mom urged.

Walking to the couch across from her parents, she sat down. She hoped she didn't look as nervous as she felt.

"You guys know James from church, right?"

"Of course, what about him?" Her father asked, suddenly interested.

"You know we know James. He introduced himself when you two became friends months ago. Stop stalling. Spit it out." Her mother ordered.

"Okay," Robyn sighed, trying to steady her heartbeat and shake the quiver that had wrapped itself around her vocal chords without warning. "Over the past few months, James and I have gotten really close."

"How close?" Her father interrupted, abruptly turning off the TV. "Where is this going?"

"Walter, honey, let her finish." Her mother admonished, patting her father's leg.

"Daddy, not like that," Robyn reassured. "But we have grown close enough to discover that we want more than friendship."

Her parents stared at her in silence.

"So, the other night," Robyn continued, "James asked me to be his girlfriend." She saw her father's jaw twitch.

"And?" Her mother questioned.

"I said yes," Robyn whispered.

"Really?" Her mother asked, sitting up. "I had no idea you were so fond of him."

"Yeah," she replied shyly. "I was afraid to say anything. I thought you would think I was being silly."

"Of course not Pookie, I remember what it's like to be a teenager."

Robyn smiled. She was both shocked and happy about her mother's reaction. However, she wished she could say the same about her father but he hadn't uttered a word.

"Daddy?" Robyn asked carefully. "Are you going to say anything?"

Her father stood and cleared his throat. "You're too young for a boyfriend."

Robyn laughed, she thought he was joking. "Daddy, you do realize I'm seventeen, right?"

"I don't care how old you are," he said sternly. "You're too young for a boyfriend." He repeated.

"Walter," her mother called, softly.

"Sharon, please. I've said all I have to say about this," he said firmly, before leaving the room.

Robyn frowned. "What's wrong with him?"

"Come sit with me," her mother said, patting the couch.

Robyn did as she was told. "What's wrong with daddy?" She asked again. "I've never seen him act like that before."

"Well, he's your father and you're his daughter. How did you expect him to react about this?"

"I don't know, happy?" Robyn shrugged. "Or, at least willing to talk about it."

Her mother smiled. "Tell me, why does James have to be your boyfriend?" She asked.

"Nailed it!" She confirmed to herself, thinking about her notes. "Because I like him more than just a friend," she answered.

"I know you like him. I want to know why the relationship has to be labeled?"

"That's what people do when they really like each other and the word friendship no longer suits the relationship."

"I didn't ask you about what others do; I asked why do you have to do it?"

Robyn sighed. She didn't understand the point of the question. "Well, James is the only guy I like, the only guy I want to get to know, and the only guy I want to spend time with. So, that makes him my boyfriend."

"Okay," her mother responded. "So, why can't James be all of that to you and you be all of that to him without the label?"

"How will other people know I'm his girlfriend and he's my boyfriend without the labels?" Robyn asked pointedly.

"People will know because they'll see how much time you spend together, how much you talk about each other, and how you treat one another," her mother explained gently. "Besides, those labels don't carry much meaning or power nowadays. Just look at Tanisha and Greg."

"I would have never told her about them if I knew it would be used against me," Robyn thought.

Robyn still didn't understand the point her mother was trying to make but she let it go. After all, things may not have turned out the way she'd planned but her mission had been accomplished. Her parents knew she and James had become more than friends and that's all that mattered. "Okay, mom, whatever you think is best," she conceded.

"That's what I like to hear," her mother replied with a smile, brushing Robyn's cheek with the back of her hand. "And don't worry about your father, I'll talk to him."

"Thanks mommy," Robyn cheered, kissing her mother's cheek, leaving the room with confidence.

CHAPTER FIVE

A friend loves at all times, and a brother is born for a time of adversity.
– Proverbs 17:17 (NIV)

Robyn walked towards her locker the next morning feeling less confident about her mother's reassuring words the night before.

"I'll talk to him," she remembered her mom saying. *"I guess she didn't have much success."* Robyn concluded. *"Daddy didn't say much to me on the way to school."*

The tension had been so thick even Renee was unusually quiet. When Robyn tried to ease the tension with small talk, her father responded with a one-word answer or a grunt. He'd made it very clear he wasn't in the mood to talk.

Distracted by her own thoughts, Robyn barely noticed the small crowd gathered in the middle of the hallway. Stepping closer, she wondered aloud, "What's going on?"

Immediately, she spotted the scene holding everyone's attention. Tanisha and Greg were standing in the middle of the crowd in a standoff.

Clearly disturbed, Robyn raved inwardly, *"I am so sick of them; I'm tempted to ignore them and walk the other way."*

However, her conscience wouldn't allow it.

"Ugh," she groaned loudly, walking toward the mounting debacle.

From what Robyn could interpret, despite the sob gradually choking Tanisha's voice, she was yelling at Greg for not calling her back last night and then trying to avoid her at school this morning.

"Hey Robyn," Greg called, spotting her in the crowd "Please get your girl, she's trippin'."

"I don't need anybody to get me," Tanisha shrieked, interrupting Greg's plea. "Just answer my question, why do you keep hurting me like this?"

Slipping beside Tanisha, Robyn whispered, "Tee, maybe y'all can talk about this another time. People are staring."

"I don't care," Tanisha declared, looking pointedly at Greg. "I want to do this now. I can't take it anymore!"

"I don't know what you mean and I really don't have time for this," Greg replied nonchalantly. "If I would've known you'd be like this, I would've never slept with you. It's definitely not worth all this drama."

"Oooo!" The crowd responded in unison.

"Really Greg?!" Robyn shouted.

"You are disgusting!" Tanisha yelled too, raising her right hand as if she intended to slap him.

Greg caught her arm mid-swing.

Fear covered Tanisha's face.

Terrified about what might happen next, Robyn wanted to say something...anything. Except, she was afraid she'd only make matters worse.

However, she was ready to jump on Greg if she had to, thinking to herself, *"I don't care what Tee does, he won't put his hands on her."*

"G," one of Greg's friends called from the crowd, "Forget her, there's plenty more like her."

That comment seemed to encourage Greg because he began smiling mischievously. "We're done," he declared to Tanisha, letting her arm go.

"No," Tanisha pleaded, reaching for Greg as he walked past her. "Baby, I'm sorry. You're right, I'm trippin'; I'll change, I'll do better," she cried, going after him.

Stepping in front of her, Robyn declared angrily, "Tee! Are you serious? It's over! He did you a favor. You're better off without him. Please, just move on."

"No! I'm nothing without him, I need him," Tanisha sobbed, stepping backward. "He just needs time to cool off," she said, still looking in the direction Greg had left. "It'll be okay, I'll take care of it."

Robyn was dumbfounded. Stepping aside, she let Tanisha go. However, she refused to turn around to watch her run after Greg, again. Somewhere along the way Tanisha had lost herself and attached her self-worth to Greg.

Robyn recognized it because that was her five years ago. Since that horrible first day of sixth-grade, she'd been willing to do almost anything to not feel that type of humiliation again. Since then, she'd learned she was unconsciously trying to distract others from seeing what she lacked, self-esteem.

Robyn winced at the thought. Thankfully, she'd reinvented her image before starting her freshman year in high school.

Still, no matter how far away those memories seemed, they still affected her. Although she was no longer in the same place, she still struggled with her self-esteem from time to time.

"More often than I'll ever admit," she thought. Straightening herself, Robyn walked toward her locker.

"What are you doing over here?" Robyn asked, seeing Renee hurrying toward her.

55

"Everybody was talking about the showdown," Renee answered, pointing at the people still lingering where the standoff had taken place. "I came to see for myself."

"It was so embarrassing."

Frowning, Renee held her head to the side and asked, "Why are you embarrassed? Greg isn't your boyfriend."

"I know, but Tee is my friend. She doesn't have the common sense right now to be embarrassed so I'm embarrassed for her. I should've ignored them and walked in the other direction."

"No, you were doing what we were taught to do. Mommy and daddy taught us to help those in need, especially those we call friends. I'm sorry it didn't work out the way you hoped."

Shrugging, Robyn conceded, "Yeah, me too."

"Well, let me get back to my building," Renee said, turning to leave. "School starts in three minutes," she announced over her shoulder.

"Shoot!" Robyn shouted, walking the other way. She still needed to go to her locker to grab a book for first period.

Opening her locker, Robyn snatched her history book from her backpack and replaced it with her math book. Then, she grabbed her math notebook and calculator before slamming the locker shut.

Robyn hated beginning her days with math but it meant she didn't have to worry about it for the rest of the day. Although she did well in math, her favorite subject was English. Writing and public speaking were among her list of natural abilities.

"Oh!" Robyn yelped, her cell phone vibrated in her back pocket.

Pulling the phone from her pocket, she swiped the screen to wake it up. It was a text message from her father. He never texted her, he always called. In fact, he'd refused to learn how to text, insisting that there was no need for it.

"It must be serious," she reasoned, touching the notification to read the text.

> DADDY: I hope you're not in class yet. Let's talk when you get home. Have a good day Pookie.

Robyn read the text again. Biting her lip, she put the phone on silent and dropped it into her backpack. She walked into class just as the first bell rang.

CHAPTER SIX

A merry heart doeth good like a medicine: but a broken spirit drieth the bones.
– Proverbs 17:22 (KJV)

"Are there any more questions?" Mr. Hughes asked the class, turning off the projector.

"No," Robyn mumbled under her breath, checking the time on her cell phone. She hoped it was time for lunch.

She was right, five more minutes.

Pushing the power button to put the phone back to sleep, it immediately woke up again- another text message.

Rolling her eyes, Robyn supposed, *"It must be the girls, I know they're trying to figure out what we're doing for lunch but I won't be joining them. I'm still mad about yesterday and even if I was considering changing my mind, Tee made things worse."*

After the public display of foolishness between Tanisha and Greg that morning, she'd decided to eat lunch with some of the other girls from the cheerleading squad.

"I know I'm probably just using them to avoid the girls but I'm not ready to face them. This isn't like the other times we've had disagreements. This hurts more. If they call or text, maybe I won't ignore them. I'll just tell them I made other plans for lunch." Robyn thought to herself.

Tapping the text message icon, Robyn opened the text. It wasn't from any of the girls, it was from James.

JAMES: Come to the parking lot

The sudden flutter in her stomach caused a tiny gasp to escape her mouth, *"Oh my God, he's here?"*

59

"Is something wrong, Miss Cooley?" Robyn heard, bringing her back to reality.

"Huh?" Robyn answered, looking up in surprise.

"Is something wrong?" Mr. Hughes repeated.

"No," Robyn replied, trying her best to sound convincing.

Expressing his frustration with a downturned smile, Mr. Hughes responded, "Mm-hmm."

Smiling sheepishly, Robyn did her best to appear normal despite the fluctuation of emotions stirring within. Thankfully, the smile seemed to do the trick because Mr. Hughes finished his final announcements then dismissed the class.

Grabbing her things, Robyn ran out of class to the bathroom with purpose. If James was at her school, she had to see what she looked like before she saw him.

Moving quickly to claim the largest stall, she used the restroom, washed her hands then checked her face in the mirror. Now she understood why she took the extra time to get ready this morning. Checking herself out, Robyn's inward thoughts became clear as she looked in the mirror. *"Thank God I used extra gel before pinning my hair up this morning, no stray hairs out of place."*

She added a little lip gloss to her lips for volume and definition, took a bottle of perfumed lotion from her backpack and put some on her neck, hands, and above both armpits, just in case.

"Thanks for the trick mommy!" She silently praised, taking another glance in the mirror.

Satisfied with her appearance, Robyn hesitated, to calm last-minute jitters before walking to the school's loading zone that led to the parking lot.

Appearing at the right place at the right time…there was James, sitting in the passenger seat of a black SUV Robyn didn't recognize, parked at the curb.

The driver was nowhere in sight.

"There she is," James smiled, getting out of the truck.

Walking towards him, Robyn's cheeks warmed, "What are you doing here?"

Grabbing her backpack from her shoulder, he put it on the floor of the front seat. "Get in," he ordered with a smirk.

That smirk made her move as instructed. Nearly jumping into the passenger seat, she asked, "Where are we going?"

"Nowhere," he answered, climbing into the driver's seat. "I'm just going to park the car so we don't draw any unwanted attention."

"Good thinking," she agreed. *The last thing I need is for the resource officer, mommy's high school classmate, to see me.*

Starting the engine, James drove the truck to an empty parking spot in the back of the lot.

Watching James lower the windows and shut off the engine, she asked again, "So, what are you doing here?"

"I wanted to see you."

Turning abruptly to face the window, she tried her best to hide her blush.

"Aren't you glad I'm here?"

"Of course," she said, turning to face him. "I was just wondering what made you come today, that's all."

"Well, my homeboy Darius, this is his truck, he was coming out here to see his girl. So, I told him I'd ride because I wanted to see mine too."

Turning to face the window again, Robyn chewed her lip, hoping to relax her jaw and stop the blush threatening to return.

"Are you going to look out the window the whole time?" James asked. "I came all this way to see you and you don't even want to look at me?"

"That's not true," Robyn giggled, feeling relaxed enough to face him again.

"Really? Because that's what it seems like to me," he smiled. "You'd think a man could get a little eye contact after surprising his girl, right?"

Ready to turn her face to the window again, James stopped her with a gentle stroke on the chin.

"Enough of that," he ordered, looking into her eyes. "I want to see you. I've been picturing this moment since the night you agreed to take our friendship to the next level. Don't ruin it for me."

"I'm sorry. I'm not usually like this with guys but you," shrugging, she exhaled, "I don't know what it is."

"I get it. This is different for me too," James agreed. "You have my nerves all over the place."

"I'm sorry," she said, trying to stifle a giggle. "Sometimes you're so blunt it makes me uncomfortable other times it makes me laugh."

"Well, I guess it's worth my ego taking a hit as long as it makes you relax. Whatever it takes." James grinned.

Robyn's jaws were beginning to hurt from all the blushing and smiling, she thought changing the subject might slow things down a bit, "So, how is your day going so far?"

"It's been good so far, but of course, now, it's even better." He smirked.

Smiling from ear-to-ear, Robyn replied, "Glad to hear it."

"What about your day?" James inquired.

"It didn't start off so great. Tee and Greg had a huge fight in front of everyone before school even started."

Robyn decided that was all she was willing to tell James about her day so far, her mind wandering to her dad, *"I'm not ready to tell him about the tension between me and daddy. I already feel pathetic because I told mom and dad about us and we haven't been official even a week."*

"Never knew a dude who argued so much," James was saying, shaking his head.

"Well, honestly, it's mostly Tee."

"That's too bad, she's going to look back and regret all the time she wasted with him."

"I know; I wish I could save her from that." Robyn confessed.

"It's not your job to save her, just keep being her friend. Now, enough of that," he said swatting the air. "Darius and I have to leave soon and I don't want to waste our time talking about other people." James declared.

"Okay."

"Since we made our relationship official, I told you I've been wondering what it would be like to be together for the first time," James said, grabbing her hand.

"And?" Suddenly feeling a surge of confidence, she looked into his eyes and intertwined her fingers with his.

James, obviously caught off guard by the act, opened his mouth a little and pulled his gaze away from hers to look at their hands.

"It's great so far," he beamed, bringing his eyes back to meet hers. "Everything I imagined it to be. There's just one thing."

"What's that?" Robyn asked.

"This," he breathed, leaning in to kiss her.

Robyn fell limp against him, closing her eyes, enjoying the moment. His lips fit perfectly against hers.

The world spun quickly behind her eyelids as she lost herself in the kiss. Her body, no longer under her control, stilled as her lips moved instinctively against his.

Seconds later, James pulled away.

"Robyn?" He called gently, stroking her cheek with the back of his hand.

"Yes," she answered, her eyes fluttering open.

He smiled.

She smiled back, leaning into his hand.

James' cell phone buzzed, breaking the silence.

Still reeling from the kiss, Robyn exhaled the breath she'd been holding. The kiss took her completely by surprise. Of course, she knew it would happen eventually but she had no idea it would happen today.

Checking his phone, James answered.

Grateful for the interruption, Robyn turned to the window, screaming in her head, *"Oh my God, my first kiss!"* She gushed. *"It was better than I imagined, better than I expected. For a moment, I'd forgotten where we were and didn't care who saw us. It was actually breathtaking. Yeah, that word sums it up. It wasn't too wet, too dry or too sloppy. It wasn't too aggressive or too innocent either. It was perfect."*

Wanting to relive the moment again, Robyn licked her lips, savoring the now distant tingle left from the contact with James' lips.

Sucking his teeth, James dropped his phone in his lap.

"What's wrong?" Robyn asked, sitting back in her seat to face him.

"Darius is ready. We need to get back to school before sixth period begins."

Twisting her lips in disappointment, she said, "Okay." Despite the disappointment, she was also thankful. She wasn't sure she could stand to be alone with James a moment longer.

"So?" James asked, shifting in his seat.

"What?"

"How was it?"

"How was what?"

"Are you really going to make me spell it out?" James sighed.

"If you want an answer," Robyn smiled, pursing her lips. She enjoyed the few fleeting opportunities she had the upper hand. It always made her feel unusually confident.

"How was this?" He asked, brushing his lips against hers again.

"There goes my upper hand," Robyn thought swallowing hard. His touch sent a current throughout her body that settled in her toes.

With a quivering voice, she replied, "It was perfect, just like the first one."

"I agree, better than I imagined."

"Imagined? What else have you been imagining?"

"Trust me, you don't want to know." He said frankly, starting the truck.

Settling into a comfortable silence, James backed out of the parking space and drove back to the loading zone. Their time together was coming to an end.

"Well, there's Darius," James said, putting the truck in park and pointing over Robyn's shoulder.

Looking in the direction James pointed, Robyn didn't recognize Darius but the girl he was with was all too familiar.

"Jelena?" Robyn asked with disgust.

"Huh?"

"The girl Darius is with, her name is Jelena. We're in the same circle but I didn't know she had a boyfriend." Robyn concluded with a glare.

"Umm, I never said Darius had a girlfriend." James stated.

"No," she replied, turning to face James. "You said he came to see his girl."

"Yes, that's two different things."

"Really?" She asked, confused. "You've called me your girl too. Does that mean…" Robyn's voice trailed off.

"Stop," he said, holding up his hand. "When I call you my girl, it's because I mean it and it's short for girlfriend. Guys use that term for different reasons. Whatever Darius has going on is different than what you and I have. He uses it for one reason, I use it for another," James explained.

"Okay," Robyn replied.

"Okay as in you understand or okay as in I-don't-care-what-you-say-all-guys-are-alike?" James remarked.

"Okay as in I understand," Robyn assured with a giggle.

"Good," he said opening the door. "Don't try me like that again," he sneered before slamming the door shut.

"He is something else!" She thought, watching him walk around the front of the truck to open her door.

Sliding out of the truck gracefully, Robyn was mindful that Darius and Jelena were now watching her every move.

"C'mon, give me a hug. We really have to go," James said, nodding toward Darius, who was now walking behind the truck to the driver's side.

Robyn looked over her shoulder to see Jelena standing on the curb with her mouth gaped open.

Robyn rejoiced on the inside, *"I'm glad she's here, she can go back and tell the others how much of a "church boy" James really is."*

"I'll see you later," James said, interrupting her thoughts as he pulled her into an embrace and wrapped his arms around her waist.

Impulsively, Robyn threw her arms around his neck, aware that Jelena was still watching.

The truck started abruptly, drawing them from their world and back to real life.

"I'll talk to you later," James whispered in her ear.

"I'm glad you surprised me, you made my day."

"Glad to hear that," he beamed, before pulling from their embrace. He kissed her lips again then hopped into the passenger seat. Darius put the truck in drive and they drove away.

"If he wasn't in such a rush I would've given Jelena a real show. I would've shown her what Miss Priss can do." Robyn stood on the curb thinking as she watched the truck disappear.

"Is that James?" Jelena exclaimed.

"Oh, so now you're interested," Robyn wanted to say, rolling her eyes. Although she didn't have anything to say to Jelena, she knew she couldn't just walk past her without a word.

"Hello?!" Jelena said, singing. "I know you hear me, was that James?"

"Yes, that was James." Robyn finally answered, turning to face Jelena.

"Well, he's cute."

Robyn considered replying but she couldn't tell if Jelena was being sarcastic or not.

"I'm serious," Jelena said, reading Robyn's mind. "He doesn't look like a "church boy" to me."

"Duh!" Robyn thought, relaxing a little. "What did you think he would look like?" She asked, walking towards Jelena.

"I don't know," Jelena shrugged. "Maybe glasses, a starch-ironed collared shirt tucked into black church pants with a crease, thick black socks and black loafers with his hair shaped into a short afro with a sharp edge."

"Eww," Robyn frowned, picturing the image.

"And I was sure he would be carrying a Bible," Jelena added.

"I think I should be offended," Robyn replied, placing her hands on her hip.

Laughing at her description, Jelena admitted, "I guess I was way off."

"Mm-hmm," Robyn gloated, brushing the imaginary dirt off her jeans. "I'll take that apology now."

"I was wrong about James but I still think you're Miss Priss."

"I guess that's the best I'll get," Robyn said, shaking her head. "I didn't know you had a boyfriend."

"He's not my boyfriend."

"James told me that Darius calls you his girl," Robyn added, hoping Jelena would explain.

"So?"

68

"So, why would he call you his girl if you aren't really his girl?"

"It's not a big deal. It's just a figure of speech."

"As much as we talk about guys, I've never heard you mention Darius before. Do the other girls know about him?"

"No, and I want to keep it that way."

"Why? If you have a good thing going with this guy, why wouldn't you want to tell us?"

"Are you hungry?" Jelena asked abruptly. "I need to grab a snack. Fifth period starts in five minutes."

"Yeah, I guess I could use a snack too," Robyn answered, accepting the conversation had been intentionally redirected.

"Good," Jelena sighed, with a look Robyn interpreted as relief.

Walking to the cafeteria alongside Jelena, Robyn thought, *"Something isn't right. Guys don't just give titles to girls. Jelena must be doing something or has done something to deserve the title. Mmm, what is she up to?"*

CHAPTER SEVEN

A time to love, and a time to hate; a time of war, and a time of peace.
– Ecclesiastes 3:8 (KJV)

"Robyn, hold up!"

Turning on her toes, Robyn saw Tanisha rushing toward her and thought, *"Ugh! I purposely changed in the back of the locker room. I was trying to avoid her. I did well all day, until now."*

Clearing her throat to be sure her voice seemed normal, Robyn spoke up, "Hey Tee."

"I've barely seen you today," Tanisha said, catching up.

Staring blankly at Tanisha, Robyn's insides were fuming, *"Duh! I'm surprised you even noticed with your eyes clouded by your obsession with Greg."*

"I-I wasn't sure you were coming to practice," Tanisha stuttered, looking at the ground.

"You know Coach would have a fit if I missed practice this close to the competition," Robyn replied, shifting her cheerleading bag on her shoulder.

"Yeah, she would," Tanisha said, looking around the room.

"I better go," Robyn stated, ready to leave the awkward conversation. "I don't want to run laps for being late."

"Yeah, we better go." Tanisha confirmed.

Robyn walked toward the locker room exit as Tanisha followed in silence. Reaching the door, Robyn grabbed the handle but Tanisha jumped in front of her, preventing her from going further.

"Tee, what are you doing?" Robyn asked, becoming somewhat irritated. "We're going to be late."

"Then I'll make this quick," Tanisha said. "I just wanted to say I'm sorry about this morning," she shrugged. "I don't know why I spazzed on you, you were just trying to help."

"It's cool," Robyn sighed, her mood somewhat softening. "You know I love you no matter what and as much as it hurts, I'm learning there are some battles you have to fight on your own."

"Well, you don't have to worry about the battle between me and Greg anymore. We made up at lunch," she said with a wink.

Shaking her head, Robyn realized what Tanisha meant. It was the way Tanisha always got back onto Greg's good side…sex.

"Great," Robyn said dryly. "Can we go now?"

"That's it?"

"Should there be more?"

"I know there's more."

"Okay, you got it," Robyn answered, the irritation she felt moments ago quickly resurfaced. "I really thought this morning was it for you and Greg. I was sure after the way he embarrassed you in front of everyone, and I do mean everyone. I was positive that humiliating display of disrespect was going to push you to finally leave him alone," she explained. "I mean, how could he be anymore disrespectful? Tell me, what does he have to do for you to realize he's no good and he doesn't love you?"

"Contrary to what you believe, I wasn't embarrassed," Tanisha replied snidely.

"You should've been," Robyn countered, "I was embarrassed for you."

"I don't know why; every couple argues."

"That's what you call an argument?" Robyn asked, shaking her head in disbelief. "Wow."

"Yes, that's how we argue," Tanisha repeated.

"Tee that was not an argument!" Robyn shouted. "An argument is a disagreement about an issue with opposing sides."

"Really?" Tanisha questioned, folding her arms. "I know the definition of an argument."

"If you did, then you would know that mess between you and Greg this morning was not an argument," Robyn explained. "The way he insulted you, criticized you, and disowned you in front of everybody, that was almost verbal assault. Oh and speaking of assault, we almost came to blows with him! That doesn't typically happen in an argument."

"You'll see," Tanisha huffed. "Everyone isn't going to understand you and James either. They won't understand your relationship or why you're attracted to him. But as long as y'all love each other…"

"That's not love Tee!" Robyn exclaimed, interrupting Tanisha's twisted explanation.

"Well, that's our definition of love. That's how we express our feelings."

"Then, I'm sorry. You don't know what love is," Robyn said sadly.

"Look," Tanisha said firmly, raising her finger. "I shouldn't have to defend my relationship to my best friend."

"I wish you understood how much you really deserve. How much you could have if you would just let Greg go."

"Robyn, you're supposed to support me," Tanisha stated. "I'm supposed to be able to talk to my best friend about everything, even if she disagrees."

"Tee, I do support," Robyn affirmed. "But I'm not always going to agree with everything you do. Because I love you, I'm going to tell you the truth when you need to hear it," she explained, stepping closer. "And right now, you need to hear the truth."

"Well, we can talk about it later," Tanisha said, stepping back. "I don't want us going into practice mad at each other. I just wanted to apologize for taking my anger out on you this morning," she said, opening the door, leaving Robyn behind.

Robyn knew later would never come. As usual, Tanisha never used common sense when it came to Greg.

"I wish I could save her but I guess life will just have to teach her instead." Robyn reasoned.

Wanting to go into practice with a clear mind, she took a deep breath. She didn't want her brain clouded with Greg and Tanisha's issues while she was standing in the hands of others, several feet in the air. Not to mention, she certainly didn't want the day of her first kiss to be tainted by the memory of Tanisha falling for Greg's games, again.

Taking another deep breath, Robyn walked into the gym just in time for practice to begin.

CHAPTER EIGHT

Happy is the man that findeth wisdom, and the man that getteth understanding.
– Proverbs 3:13 (KJV)

"Bye!" Robyn and Tanisha called to the other cheerleaders before getting into Tanisha's car. After another hard cheerleading practice, Tanisha was taking Robyn home.

"I'll be so glad when this competition is over," Tanisha huffed, starting the car. "Coach is wearing me out!"

"I know! Thank God it's next Saturday."

"So," Tanisha said, pulling out of the school's parking lot, "What are you going to do with all that free time when cheerleading is over? Are you going to fill it with James?" She sang.

"I'm not making any plans or rushing into anything. I'm just going with the flow," Robyn said coolly.

"Mm-hmm."

"He came to see me today."

"Who? James?" Tanisha asked with surprise. "Really?"

"Yes," Robyn beamed, reliving the moment. "It was a surprise."

"So what did y'all do on this surprise visit?" Tanisha asked, raising her eyebrows.

"He kissed me," Robyn confessed, grinning.

"Oh! How was it?" Tanisha asked, turning onto Robyn's street.

"It was sweet, very nice."

"Sweet? Nice?" Tanisha scoffed. "How long have y'all been friends?"

"A little over six months," Robyn answered. "Why?"

"You mean to tell me that y'all have been beating around the bush for six months and the first chance he gets to kiss you, it's just sweet?" Tanisha asked in disbelief, pulling into Robyn's driveway. "No ma'am, his tongue should've been down your throat."

"Tee!" Robyn yelped, taking off her seatbelt. "What if we just want to take things slow?"

"If you say so," Tanisha accepted. "I guess I should be happy that he even made a move so fast since he's a "church boy," right?"

"Tee, James is still a man. The fact that he grew up in church doesn't change that."

"I know. I'm just not convinced he's right for you."

"Seriously? You really want to go there?" Robyn asked, raising an eyebrow.

Tanisha shifted in her seat, sucking her teeth.

"I didn't think so," Robyn concluded, trying to laugh it off. "Besides, you can't make a decision about James without meeting him or getting to know him," she explained. "I mean, I'm not crazy about Greg now but at least I gave him a chance before forming my opinion."

"You're right," Tanisha sighed, holding her hands up in surrender. "I'll give him a chance."

"Thank you."

After sitting in silence for a few moments, the porch light suddenly came on. That was Robyn's cue.

"Let me go before Sharon comes out here," Robyn said, opening the car door to get out.

"Yeah," Tanisha agreed with a giggle. "Mama Sharon does not play."

"Thanks for the ride Tee, text me when you get home so I know you made it."

"Okay, see you tomorrow," Tanisha replied, putting the car in reverse.

"She got some nerve," Robyn thought, walking to the front door, discovering it was slightly opened.

"I'm home!" She yelled to no one in particular, closing the door behind her.

"Duh! That's why the door was open!" Renee sang from her bedroom.

"You get on my nerves," Robyn sang back with a giggle.

Suddenly feeling tired from the day's events, Robyn walked to her bedroom and fell onto the bed.

"Hey Pookie," her mother said, standing in the doorway.

"Hey mommy," Robyn replied, sitting up.

"How was practice?"

"Hard."

"Well, you're almost at the finish line."

"Thank God." Robyn replied.

"When you get settled, come see me and dad."

Sucking her teeth, Robyn thought, *"Ugh! I forgot daddy wanted to talk."*

"I thought he'd want to talk later tonight?" Robyn asked, frowning. "I just got home."

"I guess he's changed his mind," her mother said, walking away.

"Great," Robyn muttered, careful not to let her mother hear.

Unfortunately, her mother's expression hadn't hinted to what her father had to say or his mood.

Preparing herself for the worst, Robyn concluded, *"No matter what daddy says, I'm not telling James I can't be his girlfriend because my parents said so. It's too late."*

Trying to delay the inevitable, Robyn took her time getting settled. After treating herself to a long, hot shower, she strolled back to her bedroom to change into her pajamas.

Glancing at the clock, she checked the time. "It's getting late," her stomach echoing the same. The snack she'd had for lunch was long gone.

Robyn sauntered toward the kitchen, warmed up a small helping of leftover spaghetti and fixed a glass of her father's famous sweet tea. Still not ready to talk to her father, she wandered into Renee's room to eat.

"What are you doing?" Robyn asked, plopping onto Renee's bed.

"Trying to find something to watch on TV," Renee answered, glancing at Robyn from the foot of the bed. "Don't get anything on my bed," she warned.

Placing a forkful of spaghetti into her mouth, Robyn blared, "I'm not but if I did, it's not like you'd notice Miss Piggy."

"What are you doing?" Renee asked, ignoring the quip, still flipping through channels.

"Avoiding your parents."

"Why?" Renee snorted, turning to face Robyn.

"Because daddy texted me before first period saying he wanted to talk when I came home."

"He texted you?" Renee asked, wide-eyed. "It must be serious."

"I know," Robyn agreed.

"Do you know what he wants to talk about?"

"James," Robyn stated flatly. "What else could it be?"

"Maybe he's had a change of heart about the entire situation," Renee offered.

"You think so?"

"It's possible," Renee said. "You never know with daddy, he can be a big softy when it comes to us."

"Well, he wasn't soft when we were talking the other night," Robyn murmured, taking another bite. "He totally flipped out."

"I think that reaction had a lot more to do with shock," Renee said. "I mean, come on, this is the first time he's had to deal with this."

Laughing, Robyn accused Renee, "That's because you keep the guys you like to yourself."

"And you should've learned from me," Renee replied, laughing too.

With a mouthful of spaghetti, Robyn took a pillow from the bed and threw it at Renee but she missed. Renee was right.

"Why did you have to tell mom and dad about James?" She asked, scolding herself. *"James attends our church. It's not like I can be his girlfriend over the phone and pretend he doesn't exist when I see him at church. Telling mom and dad was the only way I could be honest with everyone, and especially myself."*

"Did you hear what I said?" Renee asked, raising her voice.

"No, sorry," Robyn answered, bringing her focus back to their conversation.

"I said stop stalling and go talk to them. You're going to drive yourself crazy the longer you sit here trying to figure out what dad wants to say when you could just go talk to him and find out."

Digging deep down, Robyn expelled the largest moan she could muster. She knew her sister was right…again.

79

"Get out my room," Renee ordered sternly, trying her best to appear serious.

"Can I at least finish my dinner?"

"Not in here," Renee said, pulling Robyn off the bed and pushing her towards the door.

"I can't believe you're treating your only sister like this," Robyn said, feigning offense, stumbling into the hallway.

"Whatever," Renee laughed, closing the door and locking it.

"Renee?" Robyn called.

There was no response, the increasing volume on the television was more than noticeable.

Left alone in the dimly lit hallway, Robyn realized it was better to go to her parents as she'd been instructed than have them come find her. She'd learned from her days of getting spankings that things never turned out well when her mother had to find her.

Stopping by the kitchen again, she quickly washed her bowl and fork. She'd forgotten her glass in Renee's room but since it was clear Renee was not going to let her back in, it was Renee's glass now. She would be responsible for washing it.

Turning off the kitchen light, she walked to the door of her parents' bedroom. Taking several deep breaths to calm her nerves, she knocked on the door.

"Just a minute," her mom answered.

Shifting from foot to foot, she waited impatiently for the shuffling on the other side of the door to subside. Thinking while she waited, *"It was hard enough to walk to the door and knock, now they want me to wait?"*

"Come in," her mother finally called after several minutes.

Reaching for the doorknob, Robyn discovered it was locked.

"The door is locked," Robyn whined, the dramatics of the moment only adding to her uneasiness.

"Sorry," her mother said, opening the door. "Come in."

Robyn walked into the room, heading toward the bed to sit down.

"We're going to sit on the couch," her mother said, closing the door.

"So this is a formal conversation," Robyn concluded, walking toward the couch.

They always talked on the bed. The couch was for decoration more than anything.

Sitting on the couch with her hands folded in her lap and legs crossed at the ankle, Robyn felt like she was in the principal's office waiting for judgment.

"Your father is out on the patio finishing up a call." Her mother announced, sitting beside her.

Nodding in reply, Robyn stayed quiet.

"I thought I was going to have to come find you."

"Oh, I was talking to Renee."

"Mm-hmm," her mother voiced, giving her the side eye.

"Sorry about that," her father announced, walking into the room.

Robyn exhaled, grateful his entrance freed her from her mother's glare.

Sitting down beside her, he cleared his throat.

Smack in the middle of her parents, she thought, *"Great, I'm sandwiched between the two of them. Heat on each side."*

"Robyn," her father began, "I want to apologize for my reaction last night."

Robyn's ears perked up as she turned to face her father. No way he'd just said what she thought she'd heard.

"I shouldn't have reacted that way," he continued. "I'm glad you felt comfortable enough to come to your mother and me about James. Thank you for being honest with us; it is a true sign of maturity."

"Wow," Robyn swallowed in disbelief. "Thanks daddy, just wanted to be honest."

"And we appreciate it," her mother chimed in.

"I really like him," she whispered, looking ahead.

"I knew this time would eventually come," her father said, sighing loudly. "I was hoping it would come much later but it's come now and we can't ignore it."

"What-" Robyn began.

"Let me finish," her father said, holding up his hand.

"Yes sir."

"Now," he said, sighing again. "Your mother and I have talked and we realize we can't control who you like. However, we don't want you calling him your boyfriend or him referring to you as his girlfriend. You're too young to be in a titled relationship."

Robyn's thoughts began swirling, *"I'm not going to fight that battle again."*

"Do you have anything you'd like to say?" Her mother asked, rubbing Robyn's back.

"Yes."

"Okay, go ahead," her mother urged.

Pausing to collect her thoughts and consider her tone, careful not to be disrespectful, Robyn asked, "Daddy, why did you get so upset last night? I've never seen you like that before."

Exhaling loudly, her father looked at her mother, who returned his look with a nod of approval.

"Robyn, do you know why your Aunt Karen and I are so close?" Her father asked.

Frowning, Robyn wasn't sure how to answer, she thought, *"What does this have to do with anything?"*

"Pookie?" Her father called.

"Well, I guess it's because you and Aunt Karen are a year apart and were the last to leave home."

"Yeah, that's part of it," he said, standing up. "When your Aunt was about your age she met a guy named Kenny," he continued, pacing the floor. "Kenny went to school with us. He was my classmate but I didn't know much about him. We weren't in the same circle so I didn't care whether him and Karen dated or not. I was too wrapped up in what I had going on to get to know the guy or even ask around about him like you'd think any brother would do.

Anyway, Karen fell hard for Kenny. Within a matter of weeks, things became serious between them. Still, I didn't care and your Grandmother wasn't worried because she thought it was just "puppy love." She didn't think the relationship would go any further than the schoolyard. Three months later, your Aunt came home and told your Grandmother and me she was pregnant. Even worse, Kenny had no intention of helping or even being involved. Just like that, he was through with her. When I finally asked around about him, I learned he was with another girl. He'd moved on like nothing happened."

"Wow," Robyn whispered, standing up too. "Aunt Karen must've been devastated. What happened to the baby?" She asked, looking at her father to continue.

"Here," her mother said, tugging Robyn's hand to guide her back to the seat beside her. Before continuing, she sighed, "Karen couldn't bear the thought of being in high school and raising a child alone so, she did what she thought was best. She had an abortion."

"Really?" Robyn said, looking to her father for confirmation but he had his back to them.

"I'm afraid so," her mother spoke up, pulling Robyn closer.

Still unable to connect the dots, Robyn asked cautiously, "So what does Aunt Karen's situation have to do with the way daddy reacted last night?"

"Karen was your age and in the same grade as you," her father answered, turning to face Robyn. "Hearing about James and how you feel about him brought up those old memories and stirred up some unresolved emotions. In an instant, a "puppy love" relationship evolved into something that has left a permanent consequence Karen, and maybe I, have not recovered from. I won't allow anything like that to ever happen again, not on my watch, not to my baby girl."

Understanding her father's heart, Robyn said, "I get it." Nothing else needed to be said.

Smoothing Robyn's hair, her mother asked, "Anything else?"

"What about going on a date with him?"

"Well-" her mother began.

"It would definitely have to be with a group," Robyn's father interjected.

"Every time?" Robyn whined.

"Can we cross that bridge later?" Her father asked, slightly pleading.

"Okay," she agreed, seeing the struggle in her father's eyes. *"I know he feels responsible for what happened with Aunt Karen but I'm glad he seems to accept that dating is inevitable for me,"* she observed inwardly. *"I'm just happy he's making progress. This would be a nightmare if he wasn't onboard."*

"Thank you," her father responded with a heavy sigh. "Now, here are the rules."

"Rules?"

"Yes, rules," her mother chimed in. "You can do this our way or not at all, your choice."

"Your way." Robyn replied eagerly.

"You must really like him," her mother pointed out, smiling brightly.

Blushing softly, Robyn whispered, "I do."

"Lord, help me," her father prayed.

Trying her best to suppress her laughter, Robyn asked, "Daddy, what are the rules?"

"They're simple. We want you off the phone at a decent hour and under no circumstances is he allowed in this house without our permission. The first time you break the rules, your grades slip, or your other responsibilities fail, there will be consequences. Understood?"

"Is that all?" Robyn exclaimed to herself. *"That's nothing!"*

"Robyn, do you understand?" Her mother repeated.

"Yes, I understand."

"Good," her father said before excusing himself from the room.

The air in the room suddenly easier to inhale, Robyn relaxed for the first time since entering her parents' bedroom.

CHAPTER NINE

Honour thy father and thy mother: that thy days may be long upon the land which the Lord thy God giveth thee. – Exodus 20:12 (KJV)

Two days later, Robyn snuggled into bed talking to James after an easy Friday of school and a cancelled cheerleading practice. They'd been on the phone for an hour watching a movie on TV, talking during the commercials.

"We should go out this weekend," James offered during a commercial. "What do you think?"

Feigning excitement, Robyn replied, "That's a great idea. Let me check with my mom first to make sure we don't have any family plans."

"No problem."

"Great! That will buy me some time. I can't ask mom and dad about going on a date, daddy just started accepting this whole idea."

"Ask her tonight," James said, more like an order than a suggestion.

"And there goes my time," Robyn groaned silently.

"I have to go; I need to start getting ready for church tonight. You're coming right?" James asked

"Yeah, I'll be there."

Right before hanging up the phone, James blurted, "Great, I can't wait to see you."

Robyn held onto the phone a moment longer. The second she put the phone down, she would have to leave the world where she and James were together without rules or restraint, to re-enter the world where she would have to ask her dad about going on her first date.

Glancing at the clock, Robyn grudgingly put the phone down. It was time for her to get ready for church too.

Like most Friday nights at church, tonight was pastoral teaching. During football season, Robyn usually missed Friday night services due to cheerleading obligations. Tonight, she was looking forward to church because it would be the first time she saw James since their kiss.

Getting out of bed, Robyn strolled to her closet. Deciding on a dress and a pair of wedges, she stood in the mirror to analyze herself.

"You look fine," her mother announced, leaning against the door frame.

Turning to her mother, she scrunched her face. "Are you spying on me?" She asked, trying to hide her embarrassment. She hadn't meant for anyone to see her fussing over her outfit.

"It's not spying if it's happening in my house," her mother answered with a wink. "Be ready to leave in five minutes."

"James wants to take me on a date," Robyn blurted, feeling surprisingly relieved.

Sighing heavily, her mother closed her eyes and rolled her shoulders backwards.

"Mom?"

"I heard you," her mother answered, opening her eyes again. "Your father and I can't do much about your liking James but we're not ready for you two to be alone on a date. You heard your father, it would have to be a group date."

"Don't you trust me to be alone with James?"

"Of course," her mother said, stepping closer. "You haven't given us a reason not to trust you."

"Well, don't you like him?"

"From what I can see, he seems very nice."

"So, what is it?"

"We don't trust him," her mother said frankly. "We aren't comfortable or familiar enough with James to trust him. Besides, we'd need to sit down with him before that happened so he's aware of our expectations."

"You want to talk to him?"

"Of course," her mother said frowning. "You didn't think we'd let you go out with someone without talking to them first, did you?" Her mother grunted, leaving the room.

"That's exactly what I want y'all to do!" Robyn mouthed angrily to her mother's back, careful not to let a sound escape.

———

"What's wrong with you?" Renee whispered, elbowing Robyn in the arm.

Robyn looked at her sister, shaking her head.

They were in the backseat of the car riding with their parents to church and Robyn didn't want to discuss anything around them.

Moments later Robyn's phone vibrated with a text.

RENEE: What happened??

"Make sure those phones are turned off before we go inside," their father warned from the driver's seat.

No doubt he'd heard Robyn's phone vibrate, she was sitting directly behind him. It wasn't enough to have their phones on silent; he always wanted them turned off so they wouldn't be tempted to check it during service.

Renee cleared her throat loudly, drawing Robyn's attention back to the red indicator light flashing on her phone. Renee had sent another text message.

RENEE: Hellooooo? What's up? ☹

ROBYN: James wants to go on a date

RENEE: And this funky attitude you're wearing is your response?

ROBYN: No I'm excited ☺ a little nervous too!

RENEE: So why the sour face?

ROBYN: I told mommy about it before we left. She and daddy want to talk to James first but I'm supposed to give him an answer tonight.

RENEE: Oh…

ROBYN: Mm-hmm

RENEE: Maybe it won't be so bad *fingers crossed*

ROBYN: Please. You know how daddy reacted about me wanting to date, there's no telling what he'll do when he talks to James about taking me on date.

RENEE: Poor James…

ROBYN: You're not helping!

RENEE: Sorry!

ROBYN: ☹

RENEE: What are you going to say to James tonight?

ROBYN: I have two choices: Tell him the truth or ignore him until I can convince mom and dad otherwise.

"Ha!" Renee laughed out loud.

Robyn shot Renee a deadly glare. The last thing she wanted was to draw her parents' attention to them.

The frenzied texting between the two sisters continued.

ROBYN: What's so funny?!

RENEE: I'm sorry but there's no way you're going to convince them NOT to talk to your first boyfriend.

ROBYN: It could happen...

RENEE: You watch too much TV

ROBYN: So, option two is out?

RENEE: Definitely

ROBYN: Well, option one is out too. I can't do it.

RENEE: Your choice

"Let's go ladies," their mother called from the passenger seat. "We're here."

"And don't forget to turn those phones off," their father reminded.

Stepping out of the car, Robyn inhaled deeply to steady her nerves, thinking of a plan, *"I'll just ignore James during service so he won't try to talk to me afterwards."*

It had become second nature to Robyn to steal a few glances of James while he played the organ. She enjoyed watching how he moved to the music and seeing how the music made him feel. However, she especially loved the moments their eyes met and they shared an intimate moment despite the crowd.

"Even if I do pull it off and ignore James, the minute service ends I know he'll be headed my way trying to find out why I'm acting weird," she

told herself. *"Besides, we never leave right after church thanks to mommy and daddy, so there's really no escaping him."*

Abandoning that idea, Robyn tried to think of an excuse as to why she suddenly could not attend church but her mind went blank. *There's no point, mommy and daddy would never hear of it."*

There were few occasions where the Cooley family missed church.

Robyn reluctantly closed the car door, slowly following her parents to the entrance of the church. Spotting a friend, Renee skipped ahead.

"Pick up the pace Pookie, service has already started," her father called over his shoulder.

Robyn did as she was told but not before she stopped to pick invisible lint from her skirt, thinking, *"At this point, I'll do anything to stall."*

Approaching the front steps, Robyn could hear Deacon Lewis through the speakers. He was giving his usual mini-sermon before he did what he was actually supposed to do which was, pray.

"Thank God for small miracles!" Robyn rejoiced, smiling a little too hard.

She knew she could count on Deacon Lewis to say his traditional, lengthy prayers. They would have to wait in the foyer until he'd finished so Robyn decided to sneak into the bathroom and take another look in the mirror while they waited.

Turning on the faucet, relief suddenly washed over her as she said to her reflection, "Tell him the truth."

In that moment, Robyn decided James would have to endure everything that came along with her if he really liked her, including her parents' rules.

"No matter how ridiculous they seem or how uncomfortable I may be," she murmured, gritting her teeth.

Despite the sudden surge of confidence she was feeling, Robyn closed her eyes and whispered a prayer.

"Hey," Renee called, peeking into the bathroom. "It's go time, Deacon Lewis is finally wrapping it up."

"I'm coming," Robyn answered, turning off the faucet, then reapplying her lip gloss.

Stopping herself from attempting to stall again, Robyn emerged from the bathroom and rejoined her family in the foyer as the usher was opening the doors to the sanctuary.

Masking her anxiety, Robyn held her head high, rolled her shoulders back and followed her parents into the sanctuary with Renee at her side. She walked coolly, focusing on her mother's back, refusing to look in James' direction for fear he would be staring back at her.

Finally arriving at their usual seats on the third row near the front, Robyn dared to look at James. She was right; he was staring back at her.

Smiling shyly, she quickly looked away.

CHAPTER TEN

Friends come and friends go, but a true friend sticks by you like family.
– Proverbs 18:24 (MSG)

"Ouch," Robyn flinched, groaning under her breath.

It was the second time her mother elbowed her in the rib. The first time, she'd been caught staring into space, not really interested in what Pastor Smith was teaching. This time, Pastor Smith was asking everyone to stand for the benediction.

Standing quickly, Robyn instantly regretted she'd ignored Pastor's entire message. Growing up in church, she'd learned shortly after the Word was spoken, the test would soon follow. Now, she wouldn't be prepared.

She'd tried her best to pay attention during service. She'd even tried to get lost in the music while the praise team and choir sang but the butterflies in her stomach refused to leave. Now, service was coming to an end and no doubt James would be headed her way once the congregation sang the last *"Amen"* of the benediction.

Gathering her belongings, Robyn followed Renee toward their friends in the back of the church.

As if on cue, Robyn felt a hand squeeze her shoulder from behind. She could smell the familiar mint gum on his breath.

"It's good to see you," James said, low enough for only her to hear.

"It's good to see you too."

"How do you know? You barely looked at me all night."

"Oh, you noticed?" She asked, laughing nervously.

"Of course," he smirked.

Biting her lip, Robyn turned to face him. She pulled away from her friends slightly so they could talk more privately.

95

"That's good."

"What do you mean?"

"After I surprised you the other day, I wasn't sure how you'd be when we saw each other again. I wasn't sure how I would be. It hasn't been as easy as I thought it would be to transition from friends to dating."

"I agree, it feels like there's more pressure."

"Exactly. We were much more comfortable around each other as friends. It's like we're seeing each other for the first time, through a new set of eyes." James explained.

"Yeah, that sounds about right."

"Sorry to interrupt," Renee apologized. "I think we're leaving now," she whispered to Robyn before walking away.

Spotting her parents in the crowd, Robyn realized they were staring in her direction. If she didn't move now, she knew they would come to her.

"I better go."

"No problem, I'll walk you out."

"No!" Robyn exclaimed, a little too loudly. "You don't have to do that," she said softer, looking back at her parents. They were still watching her.

"It wasn't a question," James grinned, leading the way.

"Okay," Robyn said dejectedly.

"So, what about tomorrow?"

"I don't know," she said coyly, shrugging. "I'm a busy girl."

"What does that mean?"

"It means I'll see what I can do," she smiled before leaving him at the exit.

"Whew, well played," Robyn applauded herself, settling into the car.

"Why are you smiling so hard?" Her father asked.

"What do you think?" Her mother replied. "You saw her talking to James."

"Mm-hmm,"

Catching a glimpse of her father's gaze in the rearview mirror, Robyn quickly swallowed the goofy smile on her face.

Squeezing her husband's shoulder, Robyn's mother exhaled, "Relax Walter, we've talked about this…she has a crush and that's natural. Don't you remember your first crush?"

"Uh yeah. My point exactly," her father replied.

"Honey, you're the father of daughters; you had to know it would happen someday."

"Doesn't mean I'm ready," he pouted.

"I'm sorry, honey," her mother said, rubbing his back. "It's inevitable."

Clearing his throat loudly, he asked, "Robyn, what were you and James talking about?"

Looking to Renee for support, Robyn mouthed, "What should I say?"

"Daddy," Renee called, leaning forward.

"Hold on Renee," he said, holding up his hand.

Shifting in her seat, Robyn silently thanked Renee. She knew Renee had been trying to sidetrack their father to avoid the impending conversation.

"Robyn?" Her father continued.

"Sir?"

"What were y'all talking about?" He asked again.

"The usual, you know, when two people haven't seen each other in a while."

"Is that it? Y'all were talking for a while."

"No," she answered honestly. "James also mentioned he wanted to go on a date this weekend."

"What did you say?"

"I told him I'd check with mommy."

"Robyn," her father sighed heavily, "I don't know if we're ready to let you go on a date."

"I told her we'd want to meet James first," her mother added.

"I know," Robyn muttered. "But-"

"Daddy," Renee interrupted. "What if I go with Robyn?"

"What?" Robyn spat, turning to face her sister.

Renee raised a finger to her lips. Silenced, Robyn sat back, confused.

"What I mean is," Renee continued, "what if a group of us go with them?"

"What is she doing? She is going to ruin my first date!" Robyn coughed loudly, trying to get Renee's attention but Renee wouldn't look her way.

"That way, it's more of a group outing instead of a date," Renee explained.

Watching her parents exchange silent glances, Robyn thought in amazement, *"They're actually considering it!"*

Still, no one said a word. However, her parents continued to communicate with glances that were difficult to read in the dark.

Suddenly feeling frantic, Robyn was sure she was going to faint from the increased level of anxiety surging through her body if someone didn't speak soon.

"Robyn," her mother called.

"Finally!" Her insides squealed. "Ma'am?" She answered hurriedly.

"What do you think about Renee's suggestion?"

"I think it's a great idea!"

"Figures," her father said flatly.

Clasping her husband's hand on the steering wheel, Robyn's mother delivered the news with a sigh, "Okay, you can go."

"Really?! Thank you, thank you, thank you!" Robyn squealed, bouncing in her seat.

"Now, we're trusting you will treat this group outing as a group outing," her mother explained, turning to face her. "This is not an opportunity for you and James to slip away from the group to be on a date."

"And since this was your idea, Renee," her father called over his shoulder, "we're trusting you too."

"Yes sir," Renee agreed.

"I understand mommy, I won't let you down daddy," Robyn declared.

"Okay, you know my intuition is always right," her mother reminded, narrowing her eyes. "And even if I can't see you, God will be watching."

"Got it," Robyn reaffirmed.

Finally arriving home, Robyn jumped out of the car and followed

Renee into her bedroom. She closed the bedroom door softly then flew across the room to pull Renee into a bear hug.

"Get off me," Renee said, her whining mixed with laughter.

"No, I'm never letting you go!"

"If this is how you're going to act when I do something nice for you," Renee said, struggling to get free. "I'm never doing it again."

"Whatever," Robyn laughed, loosening her grip. "Thanks for doing that."

"You're welcome," Renee answered, pulling free from Robyn's hold.

"No, seriously," Robyn said, sitting on Renee's bed. "I don't know what I would've done if you hadn't stepped in. I probably would've given up on the idea altogether."

"It was nothing," Renee gloated.

"I see I've said too much," Robyn laughed, shoving her.

"I just figured it was the best way to give you what you wanted while making sure mommy and daddy would be comfortable."

"Well, you were right. The other night daddy did mention going with a group would be the only way I could go anywhere with James. I don't know why I didn't think to remind him," Robyn said, slapping her forehead.

"Because I'm the wiser sister," Renee joked.

"Again, I've said too much," Robyn smiled, hopping off the bed toward the door.

"I also did it because I'll be in your shoes soon and I want to be sure the path is made straight before I arrive."

"I should've known!" Robyn squealed, pulling Renee into another bear hug.

CHAPTER ELEVEN

Let him kiss me with the kisses of his mouth: for thy love is better than wine.
— Song of Solomon 1:2 (KJV)

"Are you sure I look okay?" Robyn asked Renee for the third time.

"Yes!" Renee huffed. "You know I'd be the first to tell you if you looked otherwise."

"I know; I just want tonight to be perfect."

"Well, you won't see tonight if you ask me how you look again," Renee teased, looking at herself in the mirror.

"I know I'm irritating right now but I can't help it," Robyn thought, watching Renee as she finished her hair. *"What did she expect? Today is the day! I'm getting ready to go on my first date, well, group date, with James."*

Recalling her conversation with James that morning, Robyn smiled to herself. Wanting to increase the element of surprise, she'd called James that morning instead of last night to tell him the good news.

"Good morning sunshine," she sang when he'd answered the phone, flexing her upper hand again.

"Wow. You're calling me sunshine?" He asked, his voice rising in excitement. "You must be in a really good mood. What's going on?"

"I'm in such a good mood," she sighed dramatically. "I'm having a great day so far."

"Already? The day just started, it's still morning."

"Let's just say that I'm so excited about tonight that I know my day will be great."

"Oh, so I guess you have a family thing tonight after all," he said with a hint of disappointment.

"No, I have a date."

"A date? Is your dad taking you and Renee out tonight?

Robyn knew he was referring to the times when her father would take her and Renee out to dinner or a movie. But she wouldn't call that a date. That was a father spending time with his daughters.

"No, with you," she corrected. "That's if you're still interested in taking me."

"Seriously?"

"Yes."

"But last night you said-,"

"I know what I said," she laughed. "What do you say?"

"Of course! What time should I pick you up?"

"Well, there's just a few, minor details I need to tell you about first."

"Okay," he hesitated, lingering on the last syllable.

Taking a deep breath, Robyn held onto her confidence before it slipped away. "It won't just be us," she blurted out.

"Okay," he hesitated again. "Who else is coming?"

"Well, since my parents don't know much about you except for what they see at church, they're not too thrilled about letting us go out alone."

"But they're still going to let you go, right?"

"Yes, but Renee and some of our other friends from church will also be joining us," she explained, holding her breath.

"That's cool," he said after a minute. "As long as we get to spend time together."

"Of course."

"Alone," he stressed.

"Robyn!" Renee yelled, interrupting Robyn's flashback.

"Huh? What?"

"You've been worrying me about your outfit for the last hour, now I'm asking you about mine and you're not paying attention."

Shaking her head, Robyn gave an exaggerated pout. "I'm sorry, what were you saying?"

"Never mind about my outfit now, Jessica just texted me and said she's on her way."

Courtesy of Robyn, Jessica was another stipulation added to tonight's group date. It was awkward enough that her first date would be a group date so she'd convinced her parents to allow Jessica, one of the teens from church, to be their taxicab for the night because she couldn't bear the thought of having her parents drop them off and pick them up with James watching. To Robyn's surprise, her parents had agreed without a fight.

Fifteen minutes later, the doorbell rang.

"That's Jessica!" Robyn shrieked, darting from the room with Renee following close behind.

"I'll get it," her father announced.

"No!" Robyn shrilled, grabbing Renee by the hand, quickly leading them past their father and out the front door. "Let's go," Robyn ordered Jessica, who was standing on the front step watching in alarm.

"Bye Mr. Cooley," Robyn heard Jessica stammer before she pulled Jessica away from the door and toward the car. "Goodness! What's the hurry?" Jessica asked once they were all inside the car.

"Nothing, I don't want to be late for the movies," Robyn answered.

"Mm-hmm. You didn't want to hear a last-minute speech from mommy and daddy," Renee offered.

"No, I didn't. I've heard enough, I'm ready to go."

"Too late!" Renee snickered. "Check your phone."

Pulling her phone from her purse, Robyn braced herself. Her mother had texted them both.

> MOMMY: Although you both ran out the house in a hurry, I hope what we talked about didn't leave you just as quickly. Remember girls, you don't want to disappoint God. Have fun!

"Don't text back," Robyn said, putting her phone on silent.

"I'm not," Renee replied, still laughing. "Besides, she made her point, loud and clear."

———

Entering the theater's lobby with Renee and Jessica at her side, Robyn shook herself.

"What are you doing?" Renee asked.

"I'm trying to loosen up," she answered, shaking her arms at her side.

"You look like you're getting ready to get into the ring," Jessica mocked, laughing.

"Hush," Robyn said, flexing her shoulders. "Help me find the group, there's a lot of people here tonight."

"You mean help you find James," Renee corrected.

Blushing, Robyn confirmed.

"Remember, this is a group date," Renee said.

"Don't remind me."

"There's James," Jessica announced, pointing toward the ticket box. "The rest of the group is to the left, buying snacks."

"Okay," Robyn answered, smoothing her dress. Looking eagerly at Jessica, she asked, "Any advice?"

"Three things," Jessica said, holding up three fingers to emphasize her point. "One, don't do anything you don't want to do or you're not comfortable doing. Two, no means no. And three, be yourself. That's the only way you'll enjoy tonight."

Stepping in closer, Robyn whispered, "I'm so nervous. How can I be myself?"

"Okay, four things," Jessica added. "Pretend to be confident and comfortable until you actually feel it."

"Does that really work? How long does it take?" Renee asked.

"I can't put a time on it but she'll know," Jessica reassured, squeezing Robyn's shoulder.

Feeling more relaxed, Robyn beamed, "I think I got it."

"Good," Jessica said, nodding toward the ticket counter, "because James is walking this way."

Spinning around, Robyn spotted him immediately. He was wearing a casual, black polo shirt with black jeans and black sneakers. Studying him, Robyn was very pleased.

"Hi ladies," James said, approaching them.

"Hey," Jessica said.

"Hey James," Renee said, grabbing Jessica's hand, "Jessica and I are going to catch up with the others."

"Okay, we'll see you inside," Robyn said, watching them walk away. "So, what are we going to see?" She asked James.

"Well, the majority decided to see a thriller. The guys thought it would be a happy medium between an action movie and a romantic comedy," he explained.

"Sounds good to me, not too manly or too girly."

"Hopefully it'll have a happy ending you approve of."

Smiling, Robyn replied, "Yes, sealed with a butterflies-in-the-stomach type of kiss and a happily ever after."

"If the ending doesn't deliver, I will," he promised. "No matter what, this date is going to be perfect."

Deliberately ignoring his promise, Robyn asked gently, "Date? You still think of this as a date?"

"Don't you?"

"Yes, but that's my view. I thought you'd see it as us hanging out since a small crowd had to tag along."

"Any time we spend together is a date," James said, grabbing her hand. "I don't care who's with us tonight. I'm here with you, to spend time with you."

Pleased James wasn't bothered their first date included an audience, Robyn loosened up some, "You don't know how glad I am to hear you say that. Let's get some popcorn," she suggested.

Still holding his hand, Robyn followed him to the register. Studying him in admiration, she giggled as he struggled to pull his wallet from his back pocket, careful not to let her hand go.

Reluctantly, she let his hand go to grab the small popcorn and two bottles of water he'd ordered.

"I got that," James said, grabbing the bottles of water from her with one hand then snatching up her free hand with his other.

Giggling, Robyn suggested, "We should probably head inside the theater. The others are going in now."

"Let's go," he beamed.

"That smile!" Robyn gushed inside.

Entering the dimly lit theater with James at her side, Robyn spotted Renee sitting with the rest of the group in the middle section. She was happy to see Renee laughing and having a good time.

"Thank God! She'll be too occupied to play bodyguard."

"Hey, there are two seats over there," James said, pointing to a section three rows behind the group.

Hesitating to respond, Robyn argued internally, *"There aren't any seats with the group, Renee didn't save me a seat and if we don't move now we won't have a seat."*

"Lead the way," she said finally.

Settling into her seat, Robyn inhaled deeply.

"What's wrong?" James whispered, shifting in his seat toward her.

Smiling, Robyn answered, "Nothing, I'm just happy we're here."

Squeezing her hand, James returned the smile. Opening his mouth to speak, the lights dimmed, signaling the start of the previews. "Me too," he said before brushing his lips against her cheek.

Soaring, Robyn tried to put a handle on her emotions and enjoy the moment. *"You only get one first date,"* she reminded herself.

Her heart desperately wanted to enjoy being with James, but, her brain did not agree. It was busy analyzing the entire experience, filling her head with all kind of thoughts and questions.

"How does my breath smell? Is my hair still laying down? Ugh, I should've gone to the bathroom when I had the chance. What if I have to pee? Wait a minute, am I breathing too hard? Am I hogging the arm rest? Am I eating too much of the popcorn? I don't want him to think I'm greedy. Ugh, why am I eating popcorn? I probably have kernels in my teeth now. That's it, you can forget his promise. He's not going to kiss you at all, you better savor that kiss on the cheek.

I wonder what he's thinking. Is he worried about his breath too? If he's breathing too hard? How much cologne he put on tonight? Wait, did I put on perfume? Ugh, I think I forgot. Maybe I can sneak some lotion out of my purse.

Girl, focus. You're missing the movie!"

CHAPTER TWELVE

A time to weep, and a time to laugh; A time to mourn, and a time to dance.
– Ecclesiastes 3:4 (NKJV)

The movie credits scrolled on the screen. Being with James had given Robyn such a thrill, she'd missed most of the movie.

Mumbling to herself, she asked, "It's over already?"

"What? You're not ready to leave me yet?" James asked, winking. He'd obviously heard her.

Whining, Robyn replied, "No, we just got here."

"Yeah, it seems like we did. So, let's not wait long before we do it again."

Bobbing her head, she agreed, "Okay."

"Did you like the movie?"

Wincing, Robyn wanted to answer, *"Yeah, what I saw of it."* Deciding against it, she replied, "Yeah, good choice."

"Good. Let's get out of here," James said, standing with his hand out.

Returning to the lobby, Robyn slowed to look for Renee and Jessica among the crowd.

"Where are they? I'm not going to be the reason we don't make it home by curfew."

Groaning inaudibly, Robyn realized they were nowhere in sight. Neither was the rest of the group.

Pulling her phone from her purse to call Renee, she noticed a text message waiting to be read. It was from Renee.

RENEE: We're next door in the mall, in the arcade

ROBYN: Well thanks for letting me know, I was looking for y'all -_-

RENEE: Sorry, I thought I texted you before the movie ended

ROBYN: Are y'all ready to go? We need to be home by curfew

RENEE: Nope. Daddy said we could have an extra hour

ROBYN: What?! How did you pull that off?

RENEE: I called Daddy and told him the movie ended sooner than expected and we wanted some time to eat and talk

ROBYN: Wow. So, he just said yes?

RENEE: No, not at first but he gave in

ROBYN: You're my shero! xoxo

RENEE: He asked about you so y'all need to join the group at some point

ROBYN: Okay

"So, it is good news," James said.

Dropping her phone back in her purse, Robyn looked up, "Huh?"

"For the last few minutes," he began, stepping closer. "I've been standing here watching your face go from panic to shock to what now looks like, joy?"

Smiling sheepishly, Robyn answered, "Sorry. I was checking my messages; I must've zoned out."

"It's cool. I've enjoyed the view," he admired, grazing her cheek with a kiss.

Wrinkling her nose, she replied, "Thank you, but, I wish you would've gotten my attention."

"Hey, no complaints here."

Swatting his arm, Robyn giggled.

"So, where's everybody?" James frowned, looking around. "I can't have you missing curfew after our first date. That's not a good look for me."

Nodding her head, Robyn agreed, "No it's not and I would never hear the end of it. But, lucky for you, we have an extra hour."

"Really? Don't play with me," James smirked, holding his hand to his heart.

"Yep, that's what my messages were about. What do you want to do?"

"Well, I don't want to do anything else that distracts us from each other. So, let's put our extra hour to good use."

Fretting, Robyn quickly asked, "You didn't want to see a movie tonight?"

"No, that's not what I meant," James clarified, catching Robyn's hand, closing the gap between them. "The movie was great but we couldn't talk and we weren't alone," he explained. "So, that's what I want to do now."

"Talk?"

"And be alone," he stressed.

"What about the arcade?"

"No, that's probably where everybody else is headed."

Thinking to herself, Robyn silently confirmed, *"I know, that's why I suggested it. Being alone with you in some secluded area seems too risky. I'd be paranoid the entire time."*

"I was thinking we could head to the food court," James suggested, interrupting her thoughts.

"That's still risky; we'd have to be extra careful," she paused. *"Although, it'll be hard to completely enjoy myself either way with mommy's you-don't-want-to-disappoint-God warning repeating in my head."*

"You ate all the popcorn," James continued, "I'm hungry."

Swatting his arm again, Robyn gasped, "You said you didn't want any!"

"I didn't," James answered, laughing. "But I'm hungry now. We can grab a table in the food court and finish our night there."

"That's fine, but don't expect me to eat anything," Robyn pouted. "Not after the way you just talked about me."

"Aww, don't be mad; I'm just kidding," James laughed, throwing his arm around her shoulder, pulling her to his side. "Besides, I like a woman that can eat."

Pretending to be offended, Robyn pushed from his embrace and headed toward the food court.

In two steps, James was by her side again.

Shaking her head, Robyn asked aloud, "What have I gotten myself into?"

"You'll never be the same, that's for sure," James answered.

"Oh, I'm sure of that."

Stopping, Robyn announced, "I'll go find us a table."

"Okay, I'll find you," James answered, walking toward the array of restaurants in the food court.

Deciding on a table in the corner along the wall, Robyn wiped it off with napkins from the dispenser. She arranged the chairs so they could sit side-by-side, then plopped down.

"This spot is perfect!" She praised herself. *"If we're sitting against the wall, I won't have to watch my back on all sides. God forbid someone from church or anywhere else sees us together...alone."*

Yanking her compact mirror from her purse, Robyn checked her face and hair to make sure everything was still in place.

"Hair still looks good," she assured herself. *"Tee was right about using gel and water. It works!"*

Clenching her teeth, Robyn inspected them. *"Oh my God!"* She panicked. *"Look at the kernels in my teeth! I should've left the popcorn alone. Ugh! Who eats popcorn on their first date anyway? You know kernels can get stuck in your teeth."*

Freaking, Robyn used her fingernails to remove the kernels. Some were so stubborn she had to use her tongue too.

"Maybe he didn't notice it," she told herself, trying to calm down. *"It was dark in the theater and kind of dim in the lobby."* Gritting her teeth again, she panicked more, *"Of course he noticed! He'd have to be blind to miss it."* She paused, taking a deep breath, *"On the bright side, he's compassionate. If he did see it, he didn't mention it. He knew I would've been embarrassed. Although, that makes me feel even more embarrassed!"*

Standing, Robyn decided to go to the bathroom. *"Duh! I should've gone there before finding a table,"* she scolded herself, clutching her purse as she made her way through the Saturday night crowd.

"You running out on me?"

Recognizing James' voice, even with the crowd surrounding her, Robyn spun around to meet him. He was carrying a tray of Chinese food.

"No, no, of course not." Robyn stuttered, staring at the floor to avoid his face and hide her teeth.

113

"Then, where are you going in such a hurry? Did you change your mind about eating?" James asked, lowering the tray to her face, forcing her to look up. "I bought enough for both of us."

Placing her hand over her mouth casually, Robyn replied, "Great! I cleaned off a table for us, it's against the wall." Turning away quickly, she yelled over her shoulder, "Going to the bathroom, I'll be right back."

Bursting through the bathroom door, Robyn rushed to the largest stall. Locking herself in, she hung her purse on the door then turned on the faucet. Running her fingers through the water to gauge the temperature, she hurriedly cupped two handfuls to her mouth. Tapping her foot impatiently, she swished and gargled the water forcefully at the front of her mouth.

Spitting the water out, she saw popcorn kernels and other food particles she didn't recognize race down the drain.

Smiling in the mirror, Robyn was pleased with her reflection again.

Yanking her purse off the door, she reapplied her lip gloss and added a dab of lotion near her armpits.

"I don't think I smell but there's a chance this kernel situation had me sweating," Robyn told herself. *"It can't hurt."*

Unlocking the stall door, Robyn washed her hands at the sink then headed out to join James.

Scanning the food court, she found him sitting at a table against the wall like she'd planned. However, he'd rearranged the chairs so she'd be sitting with her back to the crowd, unlike she'd planned.

Bouncing toward the table, Robyn stopped before she sat down. "You rearranged the chairs?"

"Yeah," James answered, confirming what she already knew. "When possible, a man should never sit with his back to a crowd; I need to see everything."

Nodding, Robyn slipped into the chair she'd wanted to avoid. It was clear, asking James to switch seats with her wasn't going to happen.

Sighing quietly, she thought, *"Funny, I never considered chivalry as a factor in the seating arrangements."*

"Mmm," James groaned, slurping the Chinese noodles from his fork. "This is so good."

"It smells good," Robyn retorted, settling into her seat. "Where's my plate?"

"I thought you didn't want anything," James mocked.

Smirking, she asked again, "Where's my plate?"

"I didn't get you one, you said you weren't hungry."

"You said-"

"So, instead, I got you a fork," James interrupted, dragging another fork from beneath a napkin. "I figured it'd be easier to just share a plate."

Swiping the fork from James' hands, Robyn agreed, "Good idea."

"Just don't eat it all like you did the popcorn. Have some manners this time, we're supposed to share this."

Gasping in mock offense, Robyn stabbed her fork in the Chinese noodles then put a forkful in her mouth. Savoring the taste, dramatically, she closed her eyes and whined in delight.

Preparing to taste the bourbon chicken, Robyn stopped her fork mid-air. James was staring at her. "What? Please don't watch me while I eat."

"I'm not watching, just taking a moment to admire. I told you I like a woman that can eat," he reminded with a grin.

Wrinkling her nose, Robyn lifted her fork to her mouth and stuffed the sweet and savory, bourbon chicken inside.

They spent the next forty-five minutes watching people come-and-go, joking, laughing, and talking seriously. They were on the third cycle of this routine, in the middle of a serious conversation when James stopped talking abruptly.

Leaning forward, Robyn asked, "What is it?"

Nodding his head slightly, he indicated something over Robyn's shoulder. "We have company."

Whipping her head around, Robyn saw Renee walking toward them. Jessica was talking on the phone a few feet away.

Tossing a smile at James, Renee dropped to Robyn's ear. "I know you don't want to hear this but we have to go now if we're going to make it home by curfew."

Groaning, Robyn stood to her feet. She wasn't ready for the night to end. Moreover, she didn't want it to end so suddenly. But, if she didn't leave now, no doubt she'd lose track of time again.

Pouting a little, Robyn announced, "I have to go." Sensing Renee had walked away, she confessed, "I had a really great time tonight. Thank you for everything."

Standing to his feet, James clutched Robyn's hand. "I had a great time too. We're definitely doing this again." Pulling her hand, she leaned in and he kissed her. "Next time, we'll be alone. Just you and me," he whispered.

Smiling tenderly, Robyn assured, "I'd like that." Removing her hand from his, she backed away from the table. *"I just hope I can make it happen,"* she added to herself.

"I'll call you later," he said.

Smiling again, Robyn left the table and joined Renee and Jessica at the entrance of the food court.

"So? How was it?" Jessica asked.

Beaming, Robyn replied, "Except for one minor hiccup, it was perfect."

"What kind of hiccup?" Renee asked.

"It was my fault; I'm embarrassed all over again just thinking about it."

"Oh God! What did you do?" Jessica asked. She and Renee on the verge of laughter.

"Nope. I'm not telling, I'm taking it to the grave."

CHAPTER THIRTEEN

Children, obey your parents in the Lord, for this is right. – Ephesians 6:1 (NKJV)

"Life is good," Robyn said, repeating the last line in the movie she'd been watching.

Just as she loved, the ending of the movie predicted a happy future for the main characters despite the setbacks they'd encountered along the way.

Similar to the movie's ending, Robyn felt life was good. Despite recent setbacks such as her squad losing the cheerleading competition and her supervised dates with James over the last few weeks, she still thought life was good.

Losing the cheerleading competition was a hard blow. She felt like all her hard work had been in vain. She'd cried after the loss like many of her teammates but eventually found comfort in knowing she could compete again next year as a senior.

Of all the setbacks she'd experienced over the last few months, including her changing relationship with the girls, the chaperoned dates with James was the one she didn't like to think about. She'd convinced herself that if she didn't give it too much thought, it wasn't that big of a deal. Still, if she was being honest with herself and others, it was a big, humiliating, deal.

Telling James their second date had to be a movie night at her house, with her parents, was easy. She'd convinced him by stressing it as an opportunity to get to know her parents in an intimate setting.

"It was somewhat true," Robyn said aloud.

Months had passed and her parents were still hesitant to accept they were dating. They claimed they still didn't know enough about James.

119

The truth was, Robyn realized, they could never know enough about the guy who wanted to date their daughter. The other part of the problem was her father still hadn't completely accepted she was growing up and liked guys.

"I can't believe daddy's still so stubborn about this," she murmured, shaking her head.

Telling James their third date would be another movie night at her house, with her parents, was harder. Initially, it had only been hard trying to decide how she would break the news to James. However, her plan hadn't worked. Instead of agreeing, James had asked if they would ever go on a date by themselves and if it was even an option. He asked for the truth.

So, with a little insight from Renee, Robyn exaggerated the truth. She used the truth of her father not having a son of his own to convince James their blossoming camaraderie was good for her father. It was a wild declaration but it worked!

Robyn had felt like a winner. She'd also felt slightly manipulative and wasn't too happy with all the lying she'd done since they started dating. However, she'd dismissed both feelings because everyone was happy. Then, the date happened; it was almost perfect.

The movie ended a few minutes after 11 p.m. The date started almost an hour late because Robyn's father had been on a phone call too long. To make matters worst, her mother had made Robyn and James sit in the kitchen with her as she prepared snacks and appetizers while they waited for her father.

"I can't believe mommy wouldn't even let us sit in the living room by ourselves," Robyn recalled, whining. "Seriously, what did she think would happen with her in the next room? But, I guess daddy's inconsiderate tardiness should've been my first clue the night would end badly."

Robyn recalled how she'd studied James' body langauge during the movie for signs of uneasiness or annoyance. She'd figured his demeanor would show how he felt about being on a date with her parents even if he never told her. Yet, to her surprise, he'd appeared at ease.

"That was your second clue," Robyn pointed out. "He was too comfortable."

Since it was late, James had begun gathering his belongings during the final scene of the movie. The moment the credits began to scroll across the screen, he stood to leave.

"Thank you for another nice evening, Mr. and Mrs. Cooley," James said.

"Glad you enjoyed it," her father replied, reaching out to shake James' hand.

"I'm glad you could join us again tonight," her mother said. "I'm sure Robyn is too," she said, nodding toward Robyn.

Smiling brightly, Robyn wrinkled her nose in confirmation.

"I'd do just about anything for a smile like that," James declared.

Suddenly mute from the weight of that compliment, Robyn looked on in silence. Her father shifted from foot to foot as her mother stood at his side trying to mask the smirk on her face.

"As a matter of fact," James continued when no one else said anything, "I've been asking Robyn for weeks to let me take her on a date so I can be an audience of one for that smile. I'd like to take her on a date, alone, but she's been stalling."

Quickly finding her ability to speak again, Robyn said, "Oh James, we can talk about that later." Nudging him toward the front door, she continued, "You better get home, it's late."

Stepping forward, her father asked, "You have? Mrs. Cooley and I had no idea."

Stopping, James turned to face Robyn.

"James, it seems Robyn hasn't been completely honest with you," her father accused.

Frowning, James looked at her father in confusion.

"Daddy, please don't," Robyn begged.

Linking her arm with her husband's, Robyn's mother stepped forward too. "What Mr. Cooley means is that we have rules."

"Rules?" James repeated, raising an eyebrow. "No, I haven't heard about any rules," he admitted, giving Robyn the side eye.

"Yes," her mother confirmed. "I'm sure Robyn will tell you about them later."

"Thank you," she mouthed to her mother.

"Robyn, hurry up and say goodnight. It's late," her mother instructed. Turning to her husband, she pulled him toward the kitchen.

"Why am I just hearing about rules?" James asked pointedly when they were alone. "I've asked you a million times if we could go on a date and you've stalled every time. I would've left the issue alone if I knew it was never an option. You care to explain?"

"I will," Robyn promised. "I'll call you tomorrow."

"You better," James ordered with a smirk before leaving.

Sighing at the memory of last night's tragedy, Robyn still felt crushed. As much as she'd tried to avoid it, it was time to face James. It was almost 9 p.m. and she hadn't called him the entire day. No matter how much time passed, she still wasn't ready to have the conversation guaranteed to be awkward.

"Okay, this is what we're going to do," she coached herself aloud. "Whenever I get the nerve to call, we're only letting the phone ring three times. That's just enough time for James to get the missed call notification. Then, when he calls back, we're not going to answer. That'll give me another day; I'll figure out something else for tomorrow if I'm still not ready to talk."

Swiping her cell phone from the desk, Robyn dialed James' number. Dancing on her toes, she chewed her bottom lip as the call connected.

"Okay, three rings then hang up," she reminded herself.

The phone rung once. Then a second time.

Jumping up and down, stirred with anxiety, Robyn pulled the phone from her ear to disconnect the call.

"Hello?" James called from the other side of the phone.

"James?" Robyn answered.

"Hey, my phone has been on me all day so I wouldn't miss your call."

Suddenly feeling dizzy, Robyn didn't respond. *"Maybe he'll let it go for now and bring it up later,"* she hoped.

"I think you forget sometimes how well we know each other," James continued. "Remember, we were friends before this. That's why I'm so confused about why you think you have to play games or hide the truth from me now that we're dating."

"I guess we are going to talk about this now," Robyn concluded. Maintaining her innocence, she finally spoke. "I don't know what you mean."

"Right," he said with a pause. "What rules were your parents talking about?"

"It's too embarassing," she whined. "Please don't make me say it."

"The faster you say it, the faster we can move on."

"Move on? You don't even know what I'm going to say. How do you know you'll want to move on?"

"Stop stalling."

Agitated, Robyn realized she was out of options. She couldn't think of anymore tactics or games to play to avoid telling James the rules her parents laid out weeks ago. Additionally, she was afraid James would soon lose patience with her so she decided to surrender.

Groaning loudly, she muttered, "I haven't been completely honest with you."

"Yeah, your dad said the same thing last night."

"Well, you already know this is new for me."

"This?'

"Us."

"Yeah, we've talked about that before."

"Well, this is also new for my parents." Clearing her throat, she continued, "This is so new for them, my daddy would actually prefer if I wasn't involved in it, thinking about it, or dealing with it."

"What is it? They don't like me?"

"No, it's not that," Robyn quickly answered. "I think it's because they weren't prepared for this stage. And there's some family history that still affects him so it affects how he deals with this. So, I thought I was doing the responsible thing when I told them about us."

"And?"

"It blew up in my face."

"What happened?"

"Bascially, my daddy told me I wasn't allowed to date."

"But that's excactly what we're doing. We like each and we've been on three dates, that means we're dating."

"I know."

"Wow. I can't imagine what your dad must think of me."

"He thinks we're friends who like each other and occasionally hang out but without the titles."

"I'm sure he knows better than that."

"I'm sure he does too but if that's what helps him sleep at night, it's fine with me."

"Ok, so what are the rules?"

"I was hoping you'd spare me the humility and forget about that part."

"Not a chance."

Rolling her eyes, Robyn explained, "There are two main rules: We have to get off the phone at a decent hour, which we already do, and you can never come over without their permission."

"Seems pretty reasonable."

"Wait, there's an unspoken rule to."

"Ok, what is it?"

"I don't think we can go on a date by ourselves until my daddy is ready."

James remained quiet.

"Did you hear me?" Robyn whispered.

"Yeah," James answered, pausing again. "I think I can handle it."

Gasping in shock, she asked, "Really?"

"Yeah," he answered again. "I mean, I should've expected some rules. Dads who care about their daughters have rules.

Plopping onto the bed, Robyn sighed inwardly, *"He has no idea how relieved I am to hear him say that."*

"Besides," he continued, "I think your father likes me so I don't think it'll be long before we can go out alone."

"I'm glad you feel that way," she replied. *"I'm glad you're confident he likes you because I have no idea. And I'm not going to ask him either."*

CHAPTER FOURTEEN

So I say to you, Ask and keep on asking and it shall be given you;
– Luke 11:9 (AMP)

The next morning, Robyn shuffled into the kitchen, looking for a quick fix for breakfast. She rarely ate breakfast during the week but on the weekends she always starved for it. This Sunday was no exception.

Opening the pantry, she grabbed a box of cereal.

"Good morning," her mother sang from the other side of the door.

Jumping back, Robyn exclaimed, "Whoa! You scared me."

"Why are you so jumpy this morning?"

Grabbing a bowl from the cabinet and the jug of milk from the refrigerator, she answered, "I'm not jumpy. I just didn't hear you come in."

"Mm-hmm," her mother responded, narrowing her eyes. "Did you talk to James about the rules yet?"

"Last night."

"Really?" Her mother asked in surprise, raising her eyebrows. "I didn't expect you to talk it over with him so soon. How did it go?"

Sitting at the kitchen table, Robyn answered, "Much better than expected."

"Oh yeah?"

"Yeah, I think you and daddy are really going to like James. He's a good guy."

"I can tell," her mother agreed with a smile. "Any more James updates?"

Slurping her cereal, Robyn asked, "Really mommy?"

"Well, we don't have to refer to them as that but I certainly expect you to share the things happening between the two of you. That's the only way your father and I can learn to trust you and James."

"She does have a point. They're not going to trust us automatically," she concluded to herself. *"I've got to give a little, to get a little."*

"Have you decided what you want to share? Or, are you still deciding?" Her mother asked with a wink, disrupting Robyn's thoughts.

"How do you do that?" She asked, sucking her teeth.

"I just know my girls."

Scrunching her nose, Robyn continued, "Like I told you, James was cool about the rules. He said he even expected them."

"Good. That means he's sensible."

"He also complimented daddy. He said fathers who care about their daughters set rules."

"Mmm, that means he's mindful too."

"Well, that's the good part. The bad part was that, before he mentioned taking me on a date again, I told him it wouldn't happen until daddy was ready."

Folding her arms against her chest, her mother remained quiet.

"The truth is, getting to know each other over the phone isn't enough," she continued. "And no offense mommy but I can't do any more chaperoned dates with you guys. I'm afraid of what daddy may say."

Her mother didn't respond.

Biting her bottom lip, Robyn asked gently, "How long do you think it'll be before you and daddy are ready to let us go on a date?"

"I don't know Pookie," her mother finally spoke. "I can't put a time frame on something like that. You and James will have to prove yourselves and that may take time."

Frowning, Robyn sulked, "I get it."

"Tell you what," her mother said, lifting Robyn's chin. "I appreciate your honesty this morning; it's only the beginning of what I hope will continue. With that said," she paused, "I'll talk to your father about allowing you and James to hang out by yourselves one day for an hour or two."

"Really mommy?" Robyn shrieked, jumping up and down.

"I said I'll talk to him," her mother reiterated. "I can't make any promises."

Squeezing her eyes shut, Robyn said, "I'm going to pray about it; that's what you would do."

"Go get ready for church," her mother directed, laughing.

Getting up from the table, she put her dishes in the sink. "Lord, please make a way," she prayed, leaving the kitchen.

━━━━━

"Amen," Robyn sang in unison with the congregation.

Looking over at Renee, Robyn giggled as Renee sung the traditional benediction heartily. She knew it was Renee's favorite part of the service because it signaled the end.

Robyn was also looking forward to the end of service. Ever since she'd told James about her parents' dating rules, she'd felt more free and confident to be around him.

Brushing past her mother and Renee, Robyn squeezed out of the pew and into the aisle. "Sorry," she winced.

"Excuse you!" Renee complained.

"My goodness," her mother scoffed. "Pookie don't be so anxious," she advised. "You don't want to be the type of woman that runs after a man, let him find you."

Slowing her pace, Robyn agreed, "No, I definitely don't want to be that woman." Gripping the pew, she stood in place.

"That's my girl," her mother winked.

"Look, he's coming over anyway," Renee pointed out.

Shifting her focus to the front of the church, Robyn saw James. He was making his way through the crowd in their direction. Smiling at the sight of him, Robyn let go of the pew.

James smiled in return.

Watching him move through the crowd, speaking to fellow church members as he passed, Robyn couldn't wait until she was the center of his attention. She cherished their sacred minutes of face-to-face interaction since it didn't happen often.

Pushing her shoulders back, Robyn began walking to meet James halfway.

"I don't want mommy trying to eavesdrop," she decided.

As she stepped closer to the halfway mark, her father intercepted.

"Robyn, give James and I a minute." Her father said sternly, not waiting for an answer before he stood between her and James, blocking her view with his back.

Turning on her heels, Robyn fumed. *This is not happening. What could he possibly have to talk to James about now? Oh my God, it could be anything! Ugh!"*

Walking boldly back toward her mother, Robyn wanted an explanation.

"This isn't going to end well if you don't lose the attitude," Renee warned, pulling Robyn's arm to slow her pace.

"I just want to ask mommy what daddy is talking to James about."

"Do you want to be embarassed in front of James too?"

"I'm already embarassed because I have no idea what daddy is over there saying."

"You know what I mean. Approaching mommy with that attitude will be a different level of embarassment. Don't you remember the last time she got you in church?"

Touching her collar in memory, Robyn asked, "How could I forget?"

"Exactly. I thought I was going to be an only child that night," Renee teased.

Regaining her composure, Robyn let out an alleviating laugh.

"Ready to go?" Her father asked from behind.

Trying to keep the lid on her attitude, Robyn grumbled softly, "I guess."

"Sorry," Renee whispered to Robyn.

"Let's go then," her father ordered, walking past them.

"Something wrong?" James asked, appearing at Robyn's side.

"I'm a little aggravated," Robyn answered. "Daddy barged in between us before we could talk and now we're leaving."

"It's cool," James assured. "It's not like we aren't going to talk on the phone later."

Turning to glare at James, Robyn erupted internally. *"No, he didn't! He's been worrying me about going on a date and since we can't, I've tried to make our face-to-face time count instead. But he's brushing it off as if this time together doesn't matter."*

"Did I say something wrong?" James asked, stepping back.

"No, only what you feel," she muttered.

"What's that?"

131

"I have to get going," she replied, walking away to catch up with her parents. Renee had already caught up.

"Hold up," James called, grabbing her arm.

Using her hand to release his hold, she explained, "James, I really need to go. Like you said, it's not like we aren't going to talk on the phone later."

Releasing her arm, he let out a stifled laugh.

"Is he serious?!" Robyn asked herself, placing her hand on her hip. "What is so funny?"

"Whoa," James said. "You're really that mad at me? Seriously?"

"I can't do this right now; I really need to go," Robyn repeated, stepping away.

"I don't know why you're in such a hurry," James called after her. "Your prarents are gone."

Frowning, she asked, "What do you mean?"

"They're gone," he repeated.

Panicking, Robyn stood in place and looked around the church. He was right, they were no longer inside. *"Ugh. I have to get to the car quick. I don't even want to think about what's going to happen when daddy realizes I'm still inside with James."*

"You're going to hate me," James said, laughing.

Scowling, Robyn asked, "What did you do? What's with you today?"

"You know that conversation your dad and I were having back there?" James asked, pointing behind him.

"Yeah, what about it?" Robyn asked, bracing herself for the worst. *"That's it! That's why he's being weird. Oh God, what did daddy say to him?!"*

132

"Well," James began, sticking his chest out. "I told him man to man I was tired of waiting for him to be ready for us to go on a date. So, I told him I was taking you on a date *today* whether he liked it or not."

"Yeah right," Robyn said, choking out a laugh. "My daddy would've had a fit if you'd actually said that."

"You're right," James admitted, laughing too. "But he did give me permission to take you to lunch today."

Creasing her eyes in disbelief, Robyn asked, "Seriously? He said that?"

"Yeah, and to have you home by five."

"Wow, I don't know what to say; I can't believe he actually said that."

"I was surprised too," James said with a smile. "Now, let's get out of here. We've wasted enough time."

Giggling, Robyn agreed, "Yes, you've wasted enough of our time."

"I'll take that," James smirked. "So, let me make it up to you," he offered, before walking past Robyn toward the side exit.

Following his lead, Robyn said softly to herself, "Okay."

CHAPTER FIFTEEN

The young man was so smitten with Jacob's daughter that he proceeded to do what had been asked. – Genesis 34:19 (MSG)

Letting go of James' hand, Robyn slid into the chair he pulled out for her. Stepping along the side of the square dinner table, James sat in the chair across from her.

Scanning the restaurant, Robyn took mental notes of the details. She studied the spring-colored, flowered wallpaper that covered the walls, the fancy blush pink, floor-length curtains draping each window, and the nude-colored carpet comprised of diamond-shaped figures. The lighting was warm and soft, wrapping the restaurant in an atmosphere of romance and elegance. She examined every inch within her view. She wanted to remember everything about her first real date.

"How did you find this place?" Robyn asked, picking up her menu.

"Do you like it?" James asked.

"I love it, it's perfect," she beamed.

"My mom suggested it," he replied, looking down at his menu. "I guess this is one of her and my dad's favorite spots."

"Mmm, so he's talked to his parents, well, his mom at least, about me. That's always a good sign in romantic movies." Robyn thought.

"Hi folks," a waitress greeted, interrupting Robyn's thoughts. "My name is Sandy, I'll be your waitress today. Have you decided what you'd like to order?"

"I know what I want. You?" James answered, nodding toward Robyn. "Order whatever you want."

Biting her lip, Robyn scrunched her nose. "No, I haven't decided yet." Looking up, she asked, "Sandy, what do you suggest?"

135

"I recommend the shrimp pasta with alfredo sauce, the steak and potatoes, or the cajun jambalya."

Licking her lips, Robyn moaned, "They all sound so good; I think I'll try the shrimp alfredo."

"Excellent choice! Would you like a side salad with that?"

"No!" Robyn answered too loudly, remembering the popcorn incident from their movie date. "I'm sorry, no thank you," she answered again, regaining her composure."

"Okay," Sandy replied, raising an eyebrow.

Avoiding eye contact with James and Sandy, Robyn tried again. "I'll just take the shrimp alfredo and any bread you offer."

"And you?" Sandy asked, turning her attention to James.

"I want the steak, medium-well and potatoes with broccoli and I'll take a side salad," he finished, with a stifled laugh.

"I could just kick him," Robyn thought, chewing her lip to keep from smiling. *"I can't eat a salad and risk having leftovers in my teeth. He has no idea how that popcorn almost ruined our first date."*

"What can I get you two to drink?"

"Y'all have the best raspberry lemonade," James declared. "We'll take one, two straws," he said, rubbing his hands together.

Covering her hand over her mouth, Robyn burst out laughing. "I can't believe you said that. That's so cheesy."

"And old school," Sandy added, laughing too. "What do you know about that?"

"That's one of my dad's moves," James admitted, grinning. "That's how he got my mama."

Laughing again, Robyn said, "Sandy, we'll take two raspberry lemonades."

"I'll be right back with that," Sandy chuckled.

"Hey, so what's with the side salad?" James asked when Sandy walked away.

"I can't tell if he just has to address the elephant in the room or if he's just always oblivious of the elephant," Robyn contemplated.

"You acted like the woman was offering you poision," he grinned.

Trying to play it cool, she blushed, "I just answered her too loudly, that's all. Nothing else to it."

"If you say so."

Grabbing a napkin from the table, Robyn placed it across her lap. Then, reaching into her purse, she snatched her compact mirror out and placed it on her lap as well.

"I'm not waiting until it's too late to check my teeth this time," she decided. *"And I can't keep getting up to go to the bathroom so I'll have to figure out how to check my teeth discreetly while we're eating. It's going to be hard but being humiliated is worst."*

Changing the subject, she asked, "What did you think about service today?"

"Umm," James hesitated, "I thought it was church as usual. Prayer, scripture, hymn, choir selection, offering, announcements, another choir selection, the prayer of deliverance, a third choir selection, then Pastor preached, led alter call, more annoucements, and finally, benediction."

Frowning, Robyn said, "Well, when you say it like that it sounds boring."

James raised his eyebrows in response.

Frowning deeper, Robyn asked, "You think church is boring?"

"Not all church…just ours."

Leaning in, Robyn asked, "What? How could you say that? We grew up in that church."

"Okay, maybe boring isn't the word," James admitted. "Maybe routine is a better word. Since nothing new or exciting ever happens, it's always church as usual to me."

Giggling, Robyn asked, "You didn't think it was funny that Mother Green's wig was twisted after she finished dancing? When she sat back down, it was so obvious that Mother Ruth just went over to her and fixed it herself."

"Yeah, that was funny," James confessed, laughing too. "But it wasn't new or exciting, that kind of stuff always happens."

"Wow; I can't believe you think church is boring."

"It's hard to enjoy most times because it's like a job for me since I play the organ."

"But you're a member too."

"Yeah, but I'm known as "James the musician" not "James the member" like you. I just see things differently, that's all. But enough about that, I can see now this subject will ruin our date if we continue," he grinned, sitting back in his chair.

"Is it that obvious I'm a little bothered by what he said?" Robyn asked herself. *"We've been talking for months and I never knew we had such different views about our church. That was one of my selling points about why I should date him, the fact that we go to the same church,"* she recalled. *"Wait a minute. Don't overthink it, don't overreact, at least not today. Enjoy the moment."*

Straightening herself in the chair, she finally responded, "You're probably right."

"Two raspberry lemonades, two straws," Sandy returned, breaking the awkward tension.

"Thank you," Robyn giggled, removing her straw from its wrapper.

"Yes, thank you," James echoed.

"No problem," the waitress answered. "The food will be out soon. Let me know if you need anything," she added before walking away.

"Everything okay?" James asked.

"It is now," Robyn answered, taking a sip of her drink.

"Good, that's what I like to hear."

"So," Robyn started, setting her glass back on the table, "how's the college stuff going?"

"I think I've finally got a plan."

"Good! What did you decide?"

"I'm going to stay here and go to community college to major in business."

"Wow, I wasn't expecting that," Robyn thought. *"That plan sounds bittersweet. On one hand, I'm happy he'll still be in town. I actually never considered the possibility he could go away for college. I always assumed he would stay here. But on the other hand, he's majoring in business! Let's be honest, he's not interested in school now; business is going to be tough."*

"What about music?" Robyn asked carefully. "You said that was your passion."

"It is my passion, I'm still going to do music," he reassured. "I'm going to do it on the side though, I'm hoping I can start doing other gigs after graduation."

"How did your parents take it when you told them about your plan?"

"They were excited. They thought it was the best plan for me," he explained. "Actually, it was kind of a family affair. We were sitting at the kitchen table talking and I decided to open up to them about how hard it was to decide. Then, I called my brother and sister because I wanted their opinions too."

"That's nice," Robyn lied.

"Yeah," James continued, "I'm just glad it's out of the way. I'm going to start working on my college application soon."

Robyn couldn't put her finger on it but she was suddenly irritated by James' parents, brother, sister, and the story altogether. Maybe it was the fact that James had decided to do the opposite of what they'd talked about. Maybe it was the fact he'd decided to do something for his life to please others. Or, maybe it was the fact his family didn't seem to have a clue about him or what made him happy.

"So, maybe irritated isn't the right word," she corrected herself, *"maybe sad or disappointed is a better word. They seem to have their idea of who James is but not the reality of him."*

Forcing herself to smile, Robyn said, "I hope you know what you're doing."

"I do," James answered.

"Then, that's all that matters."

Moments later their lunch arrived and they settled into eating. Robyn discreetly checked her teeth between bites.

Since the conversation had grown serious before lunch, they were happy to keep the conversation light and humorous as they ate. They talked about the recent episodes of the shows they loved, movies they wanted to watch while talking on the phone, and movies they wanted to see in the theater. As usual, they teased each other about their differences such as James' obsession with court TV shows versus Robyn's obsession with reality TV shows.

"Yes! Now this is the James I like," Robyn thought to herself, happy things had turned around. *"I needed this date to have a happy ending. I would've been so upset if things didn't end on a high note."*

"Are you ready to go?" James asked, interrupting her thoughts.

Shaking her head, Robyn asked, "Go?"

"Yes," James answered, looking at his watch. "It's four-thirty. Your father asked me to have you home by five. I want to get you home with time to spare. That'll be a good look for me."

Slipping her mirror from her lap, Robyn returned it to her purse. "I didn't realize it was that late."

Standing up, James pulled some cash from his wallet and dropped it on the table. Then, stepping to her side of the table, he pulled out her chair.

Taking his hand as support, Robyn said, "Thanks for lunch, I had a great time."

"Thank you for the company," he replied, brushing her cheek with a kiss. "Let's go."

The ride home was quiet as they held hands over the console. Only letting her hand go to make turns, he'd quickly grab it again. She hoped he was enjoying the silence. Every now and then she stole a glance in his direction and he was looking back at her with a smile.

Sucking her teeth softly, Robyn realized they'd arrived in her neighborhood.

Slowing the car, James leaned over and kissed her lips lightly. "I had to do that before we pulled up to your house."

"Good thinking," she agreed. *"I don't know what I would've done if you'd tried that in the driveway. Daddy is probably hanging by the window."*

Pulling into the driveway, the front door opened immediately.

Snatching her hand from James' grasp, Robyn quickly hopped out of the car. She didn't want to give her father an opportunity to walk much farther.

James put the car in park and hopped out of the car too to meet her father halfway.

"Thanks James," her father said. "I appreaciate the responsibility you've shown today."

"No problem Mr. Cooley," James responded, shaking his hand. "Thank you again."

"Sure," her father replied.

"Enjoy the rest of your afternoon," James said, hopping back into his car.

"Thanks daddy," Robyn whispered to her father, putting her arm around his waist. "Let's go inside, I want dessert."

Church Girls Just Want to Have Fun

CHAPTER SIXTEEN

...the Lord hates... A proud look, a lying tongue, hands that shed innocent blood, a heart that devises wicked plans, Feet that are swift in running to evil, a false witness who speaks lies, and one who sows discord among brethren.
– Proverbs 6:16-19 (NKJV)

Robyn was still soaring the next day. Like their date, the night had ended perfectly too.

Hours after James dropped her off, he called and they recapped their time together. They even watched a movie together before they finally said goodnight.

"So, are you eating with us today?"

Robyn recognized Tanisha's voice behind her. Turning to face her, she didn't expect to see Jasmine, Olivia, Erin, and Jelena in tow.

"What do you mean? I've been eating lunch with y'all," Robyn replied, raising an eyebrow. "I've only missed a few times because I ate with some of the girls from the squad instead."

"You're right, you've been eating with us," Tanisha agreed. "You're physically there but you're not the same."

"Yeah, it feels like you've been pulling away the past few months," Jasmine pointed out.

"Maybe I have but it's for a good reason," Robyn wanted to say.

"Yeah, what's up with you?" Erin asked.

"Every week you've seemed more and more distant. That's not like you," Olivia chimed in.

"She got her boyfriend now, she doesn't need us anymore," Jelena claimed.

"Is that it?" Tanisha asked, crossing her arms. "You've been pulling away from us because you have James and don't need us anymore?"

Sighing, Robyn finally spoke, "No, it's not like that," she corrected. "I've been preoccupied with my own stuff, that's all."

"You're too busy for your friends?" Tanisha asked.

"You and "church boy" must be real busy," Jelena mocked.

In that moment, Robyn realized she didn't like Jelena very much. *"I don't know how I tolerated her all these years!"*

Ignoring Jelena's snide remark, Robyn said to Tanisha, "I'm sorry, let's go to lunch."

That was all Robyn was willing to say. She knew they wouldn't understand that she had been distancing herself because of how they reacted the day she told them about James. She'd been too supportive and encouraging to them over the years, whether she agreed with their decisions or not. She wanted the same support and encouragement in return.

"Great!" Tanisha smiled. "We've got a lot of catching up to do."

"Yes," Olivia agreed. "I want to know what you and James have been up to."

"Yeah, you've been holding out," Jasmine accused. "I need to hear what kind of game he's using because you've changed," she smirked.

"Shoot; I might need to get a "church boy" too!" Erin laughed.

"Let's go," Tanisha ordered, lacing her right arm through Robyn's left arm. "I missed you," she whispered to Robyn, as they walked ahead.

Not sure whether she felt the same, Robyn remained silent. Instead, she laid her head on Tanisha's shoulder as they walked to the cafeteria.

"So, what have I missed?" Robyn asked, sitting down at their favorite table. *"I guess there's no harm in being social,"* she told herself. *"I've had too many good things happen to James and me to not be able to share it. Actually, this is what I've always wanted, to be able to add to the conversation whenever we talk about guys."*

"Where should I start?" Jasmine asked, looking at Tanisha.

"What?" Tanisha asked. "Robyn knows Greg and I are still together, that's no secret. So, besides our usual arguments, there isn't any news with us," she assured. "But, he has been calling every night for the last two weeks so I guess that's news!"

"Wow," Robyn thought to herself. *"He should be calling every night, that's the least he can do considering how he treats you."*

"Girl, that's not news," Erin laughed. "That's what boyfriends should be doing."

Biting her lip, Robyn tried to keep from expressing her agreement. *"Glad I'm not the only one who thinks Tee is literally crazy about Greg."*

"Maybe," Tanisha admitted, "but this is progress for us."

"Whatever," Erin replied, shaking her head. "In that case, Robyn, you haven't missed anything. Jasmine has a new friend she still isn't ready to tell us about, Olivia and I are still happily on team single, and Jelena has a new boy toy named Darius."

Robyn looked knowingly at Jelena. "A boy toy? Is that what you call him?"

"Yes," Jasmine answered. "Whatever you're thinking that is, that's exactly what she's doing."

"Whatever," Jelena said innocently. "Darius and I are just friends."

"With benefits," Erin added, rolling her eyes.

"So that's why she's just Darius' girl and not his girlfriend,"
Robyn concluded, remembering the day Darius and James had come to
visit them during lunch.

"There you go with those judgy eyes," Jelena accused Robyn.

Holding her hands in surrender, Robyn exclaimed, "I didn't say
anything!"

"You didn't have to, it's all over your face." Jelena blamed.

"I don't know what you mean," Robyn replied.

"Robyn," Tanisha interrupted, "tell us about you and James.
What's been going on?"

Grateful Tanisha rescued her from an impending argument, Robyn
smiled at her.

"Yes," Olivia agreed. "I want to know what you and James have
been up to all this time."

"Whatever it is, it must be good if you've been too busy to hang
with us." Jasmine offered.

"They have been busy," Jelena said, snidely. "I told y'all how he
came here and I saw them sneaking away to lunch that time."

"Yeah, Tee gave us some of the details but I want to hear it from
Robyn. What happened?" Erin asked.

All eyes on her, waiting for her to respond, Robyn suddenly felt
the pressure to give them a great story. *"What do I say?"* She wondered.
Deciding not to mention any details, she replied, "It was great; I was very
surprised to see him."

"Aww, he surprised you," Olivia gaped.

"Yes," Robyn said with a smile. "I had no idea he was going to
come. While I was in class he texted me and told me to come outside.
Interestingly," she cleared her throat, "James had a friend in the car with

him who also came to see someone," she paused. "It was Darius, here to see Jelena."

"We already know that," Jasmine said. "Finish telling the story."

"Oh. Well, there isn't much else to tell," Robyn said. "We sat in the car until it was time for them to leave."

"No, tell them what else happened in the car," Tanisha said, elbowing Robyn in the rib.

There it was again. The sudden pressure to tell a great- yet believable- story. This time, however, the pressure was more intense, nearly doubled.

"If I just tell them what they want to hear, they'll leave me alone and we can talk about something else," Robyn reasoned.

"We know Robyn," Jelena said. "Miss Priss didn't do anything but talk and I already told y'all about that brother-sister kiss goodbye," she laughed.

"Please shut up," Robyn said, trying desperately to prevent her simmering anger from boiling over. Rolling her eyes, she turned back to Tanisha, "You're right we didn't just talk," she said with a smile she didn't feel.

Taking a deep breath, Robyn began, "After I got the text, of course, I went to the bathroom to freshen up. When I finished, I went to the parking lot. James was waiting for me in Darius' truck, he and Jelena had already left."

"They aren't asking about me," Jelena spoke.

Ignoring her, Robyn continued, "I got in the truck and we drove to the back of the parking lot."

"Y'all stayed on campus?" Olivia asked.

"Yeah, we didn't have a choice," Robyn explained.

"One, it was Darius' truck. And two, they were on a tight schedule. They had to get back to school quickly because they had a class they couldn't miss."

"Okay, that makes sense," Olivia said. "What happened next?"

"We talked for a while about how our day had been, made plans to go out again," she lied. *"Don't worry, it's just a small lie to thicken the details,"* she assured herself.

"After we made our date plans," she continued, "James leaned in and kissed me," she lied again. *"Well, I can't tell them I was actually complaining to him about Tee and Greg so I have to make up something."*

"And yes," Robyn added, "that was our first kiss," she confessed with a smile.

No one said a word. They sat, listening intently.

"I can't tell if they're enjoying this or not," Robyn worried. *"But that's the end of the story. I don't know what else I can say to make the story longer, things seem juicier or more interesting."*

Forcing herself to continue, Robyn admitted, "I didn't expect him to kiss me," she paused. "Well, of course, I expected him to kiss me eventually," she clarified. "I mean, I didn't expect our first kiss to be in a truck. I imagined it would happen somewhere much nicer, more romantic."

"Who cares where the kiss happened?" Jasmine exclaimed. "How was it?" She asked, bouncing in her seat.

Blushing, Robyn said, "It was perfect."

"That's it?" Jasmine asked.

"Yeah, what does that mean?" Olivia asked, scooting forward. "We want details."

"What did you think she'd say?" Jelena asked, laughing. "That they French kissed?"

"Duh! Of course!" Robyn lied again. "I didn't think I had to say it."

"Oh really?" Jelena asked, scowling. "What was it like?"

"You didn't tell me that," Tanisha interjected.

"I told you, it was perfect. It's like we were made for each other. I mean, I've heard y'all horror stories and James was nothing like that," she added confidently.

"Mm-hmm," Jelena responded, sucking her teeth.

"So, how was the first date?" Tanisha asked. "You never told me about that."

"Oh, that was perfect too!" Robyn beamed. "My friend Jessica drove us to the movies-"

"Us?" Jasmine asked abruptly. "James doesn't have a car?"

"Yes, he does," Robyn replied. "Jessica drove me and Renee to meet James."

"Wait a minute," Tanisha interrupted, holding up her hands. "Renee went on the date with you?"

"Well, sort of," Robyn explained. "She and Jessica went to meet with the rest of our friends."

"So, y'all first date was a group date?" Jelena asked with a smirk. "This just keeps getting better and better."

All eyes were on Robyn, waiting for her to respond.

Trying to regain control of the story, Robyn decided to fluff the actual events once again. "My parents thought it was going to be a group date but James and I saw a completely different movie than the others," she lied. "Well, we saw bits and pieces of the movie," she said, winking with a confidence she didn't feel.

"Get it girl!" Tanisha called, grabbing Robyn's arm in excitement.

"That's what I'm talking about," Erin yelled.

Jasmine and Olivia agreed. Jelena didn't seem convinced but she didn't respond.

"After the movie, we got something to eat in the food court then I had to leave to make curfew," Robyn finished.

"Ladies, we need to pack it up," Olivia announced. "We have five minutes until next period."

"Shoot!" Erin shrieked.

"I know," Jelena agreed. "We lost track of time listening to Robyn's little stories."

Grateful for the disruption, Robyn ignored Jelena and quickly gathered her belongings and her trash.

"Girls, I have to go," Robyn stated. "I need to use the bathroom and go to my locker before class."

"Okay," Tanisha replied. "We'll catch up later."

Walking away hurriedly, Robyn scolded herself. *"Ugh. What's going on with you? Why did you lie?"* Trying to outrun her thoughts, she walked faster, almost jogging. *"And you kept lying!"*

Surprised by the response that surfaced, she mumbled, "I didn't want them to think less of me, James or our relationship. I just wanted to fit in."

CHAPTER SEVENTEEN

Truthful words stand the test of time, but lies are soon exposed.
– Proverbs 12:19 (NLT)

"Ugh! I should've stopped after the first time it happened," Robyn scolded herself, scurrying away from another "colorful storytelling" conversation with the girls. *"I said I would never let someone else's opinion affect my behavior or how I felt about myself again and yet, here I am doing it again."*

One side of Robyn didn't want to listen. That side was enjoying the sense of belonging, the sense of truly being one of the girls. However, the other side of her felt like a fraud. That side didn't like the lying, even more, having to maintain the lies she'd told to protect her cover. Unfortunately, whenever this internal battle arose, the proud side of her that refused to listen to self-reasoning always won. As a result, weeks had passed and Robyn was still lying to the girls about her relationship with James.

"Too much time has passed, it's too late to stop now," she said, trying to encourage herself. *"Is lying even the right word? It's more like improving the details or coloring the story."*

Lying had become customary, almost second nature. Since the first time, Robyn never told the girls about her and James without enhancing the facts. She'd lied about their dates, how physical their relationship had become, and even what they talked about.

Robyn had even begun creating new stories. She'd started when she learned the number of dates she'd actually had with James was lesser than the girl's standards. So, to meet their expectations, she told them about her fantasy experiences.

"I've gotten much better at this. I almost blew it a few times in the beginning," she recalled. *"But I've learned that the trick is to not give explicit details. You just give enough to satisfy. The more details, the more you'll have to maintain."*

"Robyn!"

Looking up from the pavement, Robyn saw Tanisha jogging toward her. "Hey Tee," she called, pausing to let her catch up.

"I asked you to wait for me. I wanted us to walk to together," Tanisha said, pushing Robyn's shoulder. "I thought you heard me."

"Sorry," Robyn offered, slowing her pace. "I must've been daydreaming when you said that."

"You've been in your own world a lot lately," Tanisha accused with a smirk. "It must be James."

"Whatever," Robyn responded, pushing Tanisha back.

"I'm happy you and James are doing well. I like who you are with him."

Raising her eyebrows, Robyn asked, "What do you mean?"

"Not that I didn't like who you were before James," Tanisha corrected. "It just seems like we have more in common now. In a way, I feel like he's brought us closer."

Robyn knew exactly what she meant. Ever since she'd started lying about James, she'd recognized how much closer their friendship had become.

"The funny thing is, or maybe it's sad, Tee feels closer to the fake me rather than the real me. So, what does that say about our actual friendship?"

"It's like, I don't have to walk on eggshells around you anymore," Tanisha continued.

"I didn't know you had to do that."

"Don't get me wrong, I never felt like you were judging me or anything. You just always seemed perfect, like you never messed up," Tanisha explained. "It's nice to know that you're like us. The girls feel the same way."

"Is that a compliment or no? I mean, should I be happy about that? I've always prided myself on the fact that I was different from them, right?" Robyn asked herself. *"Yes. I've even bragged that my experiences with guys were different from the norm because I'm different from the norm. So, what's changed?"*

"I just want to fit in. It's lonely being different," the familiar response tumbled from Robyn's mouth with an added truth.

"Huh?" Tanisha asked, frowning.

Clearing her throat, Robyn tried to recover, "I didn't know you thought we were so different. I've always thought we had a lot of things in common."

"Girl, stop it," Tanisha stated. "It's not that serious."

"Maybe not to you."

"Oh!" Tanisha shrieked. "When are we going to do a double date?" She asked with excitement, obviously not hearing Robyn.

"Never!" Robyn wanted to shout but she didn't want to hurt Tanisha's feelings. Instead, she answered, "I don't know if that's a good idea Tee."

"No, we have to!" Tanisha whined. "Why not?"

"The guys are so different, what would we do?"

"I don't know but we can figure that part out later. Just talk to James about it."

"Okay," Robyn answered, knowing she would never

mention it to James. *"There's no way I would ever go anywhere with Greg except class. Besides, James and I are on another level from them, that date would be so awkward."*

Choosing to remain quiet, Robyn listened to Tanisha as she imagined how their double date would be.

———

"I hear you've been holding information from me." Renee accused, flopping onto Robyn's bed.

"Hey, how are you? My day was great, how was yours?" Robyn asked with sarcasm.

"You've been holding out on me," Renee repeated.

Frowning, Robyn replied, "I have no idea what you're talking about."

Throwing her cheerleading bag on the floor, Robyn closed the door behind her then plopped down beside Renee.

"Mm-hmm."

"You know I tell you everything."

"Are you sure about that?"

"What is it?"

"Oh, you haven't heard?" Renee asked.

"Apparently not, I have no idea what you're talking about."

"Today, I overheard that you and James do more than eat whenever he comes to school during lunch," Renee said, raising an eyebrow.

Hopping up, Robyn yelped, "What?! That's a lie! Who said that?"

"It doesn't matter who said it," Renee replied evenly.

Fuming inside, Robyn said through clenched teeth, "No, it does matter. Tell me."

Sighing loudly, Renee sat up. "I overheard this girl telling one of my friends."

"Who is she?"

"I don't know her but I've seen her with Jelena before."

Putting her hands on her hip, Robyn began pacing the floor.

"Did you hear what I said?" Renee asked. "Jelena probably said something to her."

Robyn continued to pace the floor to keep from giving in to the anger she felt inside. *"I can't believe this is happening! This can't be happening! I've never said anything like that to the girls. She's lying!"* She screamed to herself.

"Robyn, did you hear what I said?" Renee repeated.

"Why is Jelena doing this to me? Does she hate me that much? What did I do to her that she feels like I deserve this?"

Robyn wanted to cry, fight and even curse. However, the truth hit her smack in the chest, nearly knocking the wind out of her. *"I can't put this on anyone but me. As much as I can't stand Jelena and I know she told that girl, I really can't be mad at her. I've never said that to the girls but I guess I've suggested it. This is all my fault."*

"Stop pacing!" Renee ordered, standing too. "Why aren't you reacting or at least responding to what I said?" She asked, grabbing Robyn by the shoulders.

"This is my fault. I should've stopped lying after the first time! I always implied and hinted at things, leaving all those blanks in my stories. I never thought Jelena or anyone else would just fill them in with whatever they wanted."

"I mean, this is Jelena we're talking about," Renee continued, shaking Robyn. "Say something."

155

"There's no way I'm telling Renee that this girl is gossiping about me because I've been telling the girls lies about me and James. It's too embarrassing, and honestly, a little pathetic."

"Robyn!" Renee called with an attitude.

"I'm okay. Things are going to be okay," she replied, holding onto Renee's wrists. "We've heard gossip about people before and most of it barely lasts a week. I'm sure there will be something else to talk about before we know it."

"Are you sure there's nothing else going on?" Renee asked, glaring at her. "Nothing you need to tell me? You know you can tell me anything."

"Oh my God! Does she already know?" Robyn freaked.

Lingering for a moment, she watched Renee intently to determine what she knew. After a minute, she gambled on the belief that Renee didn't know anything so she shook her head no.

"That's all you have to say?" Renee asked in disbelief.

"I just don't want to get worked up over this," Robyn answered honestly. "Besides, this isn't the first time my name has been involved in gossip and I'm sure it won't be the last."

"This is serious," Renee declared sternly. "We're not talking about cheerleading or Tanisha and Greg related gossip or even that old rumor about you fighting some girl in the locker room. This is bigger than all that. We're talking about sex and what people think they know about you and James. This is the type of gossip that can ruin your reputation, your character."

Moving to the edge of the bed, Robyn decided it was best to show Renee she was just as concerned about what had happened. Yet, she would have to speak vaguely about what she was going to do since she was to blame after all.

"Sit down," Robyn said, patting the space next to her.

"You're too calm, it's not like you," Renee said, sitting.

"Trust me, I'm not calm. I'm actually losing it on the inside," she admitted. "I'm just hoping things don't get too bad. And don't worry, I'll do whatever I can to make sure the rumors disappear."

"Does that include making Jelena disappear?" Renee asked, laughing.

Smiling for the first time since being home, Robyn replied, "Jelena has issues too. I'm not worried about her."

"If you say so," Renee sighed. "I'll leave it alone for now but if I hear the rumor again or if I hear anything more, I'll be confronting you about this again," she promised.

"Okay, agreed," Robyn responded, happy that the conversation was finally ending.

"Good," Renee replied, standing. "I'm leaving, I'll let you get that."

"Get what?" Robyn asked, confused.

"Your phone," Renee answered, pointing at Robyn's cheerleading bag. "I think I hear it vibrating. I bet it's James," she sang, closing the door behind her.

Pulling the bag to her by the strap, Robyn dug inside. Her phone was vibrating, it was James.

Swiping the "Talk" button to answer, she sang, "Hey!"

"Hey," he replied sharply. "What's up?"

"Nothing," she answered. "I just got home from practice, I was just talking to Renee."

"Oh, did I interrupt?"

"It was nothing," Robyn assured. *"That's right, nothing I would ever tell you about."* She thought to herself.

"Cool."

"How was your day?" She asked, sitting at her desk. "You sound grouchy."

"My day was cool until after school," he answered, clearing his throat. "I stopped by the mall for a minute with Darius. We ran into this girl named Jasmine who said she knew you."

Robyn's stomach hit the floor, her heart beating quickly. She only knew one Jasmine.

Taking a deep breath to steady her heart, Robyn asked innocently, "Jasmine who?"

"Y'all go to school together, even have some classes together," he replied firmly. "And y'all eat lunch together every day."

"Oh, that Jasmine!" She responded, in the most believable tone she could manage.

"I'm really not in the mood for games tonight," he warned.

"Did she say something to you? Is that why you're grouchy?"

"As a matter of fact, she had a lot to say," James confirmed. "Specifically, she had a lot to say about us."

Robyn's stomach flipped again. *"No, no, no, no! This can't be happening! This is not happening!"* She panicked.

"She told me things about us that I didn't even know," he continued. "She started talking about dates we've never had then gave me props about how far I've gotten with you because Miss Priss had never let any guy go that far before. I was so confused. I'm thinking, who is this girl who knows more about my relationship than me?"

"Oh my God! Why would Jasmine say that? This is not happening!"

"But the craziest part about the whole thing happened after we finally got Jasmine to shut up and leave," James continued. "After she left, Darius told me he'd heard some of the same things from his girl Jelena weeks ago."

"Just hang up!" Robyn urged herself. *"You need time to think! You need time to figure out what to say! Hang up now!"*

"Robyn, I know you," James said softly. "You've been lying about us? That's not like you so I know there must be more to this. But I can't imagine it's just a coincidence that two complete strangers know similar stories about us," he explained. "I don't know what's going on; I can't even pretend like I know. This one has me speechless. So, I'm going to give you a chance to explain and to help me understand. What's going on?"

EPILOGUE

It had been a month since James confronted Robyn about his run-in with Jasmine. Surprisingly, her father had allowed Robyn to go to James' senior prom. And his graduation had come and gone; he was set to start college in the fall.

Tidying up her desk, Robyn discovered the picture James had given her tucked away in her desk drawer.

"I still can't believe he broke up with me," Robyn whispered to her self, swallowing the lump in her throat.

The day after James' graduation party, he'd called Robyn on his way home.

"Robyn, I'm sorry but I just can't seem to forget the Jasmine situation. I really want to believe she was just gossiping like you said. But, like I've said before, it was too much of a coincedence to not believe that you had something to do with it. And," he'd paused, *"I can't be in a relationship with someone I can't trust. So, I think we should go back to being friends."* She recalled his speech like it was yesterday.

"Looking back at it now, as much as it killed me, I think he actually did me a favor. Clearly, I wasn't ready to be seriously dating," she acknowledged. "One day I'll tell everybody why we really broke up. Until then, I'll work on building the courage.

"I miss him so much, six months of dating feels like forever! I hate our friendship may never be the same but I'm grateful for what's left of it. It's funny though, I know I messed up but I have a gut feeling this isn't the end. I have a feeling we'll be together again…maybe even get married."

.

Discussion Questions for
Church Girls Just Want to Have Fun

1. Do you understand Robyn's frustration? What is her dilemma?

2. Write your personal pros and cons list for dating.

3. Why do you want to date?

4. What other methods can you think of to start a conversation with your parent(s) or guardian(s) about dating?

5. What are your dating rules or boundaries?

6. What personality traits illustrate that a person is *not* ready to start dating?

7. What personality traits illustrate that a person *is* ready to start dating?

8. Ladies, what qualities are you looking for in a boyfriend? Men, what qualities are you looking for in a girlfriend?

9. How can you formally introduce your parent(s) or guardian(s) to the person you are dating?

10. What behaviors, actions, etc. demonstrate to your parent(s) or guardian(s) you can be trusted to date?

11. Why do you think Robyn and Tanisha became closer after she began lying about her relationship with James? What does that say about Robyn? What does that say about their friendship?

12. Do you want your peers to think you're different from them or just like them? Why?

13. What advice would you give Robyn to help her resolve all the confusion she created by lying?

www.ingramcontent.com/pod-product-compliance
Lightning Source LLC
Chambersburg PA
CBHW050751250626
47155CB00005B/2009

9780998737508